The 2016 Writivism Anthology

Sundown and other Stories

Edited by Emmanuel Sigauke

Short Fiction, Poetry and Non-Fiction by 22
emerging writers living in Africa.

The 2016 Writivism Anthology: Sundown and Other Stories

First published in South Africa by Black Letter Media (Pty) Ltd
(2017)

P.O. Box 94004
Yeoville
2143

www.blackletterm.com
info@blackletterm.com

Design & Layout by Joshua Rukundo

Edited by Emmanueal Sigauke

Copy Edited by Nicola Rijsdijk

For permissions to use, sales info and other queries - info@
blackletterm.com.

ISBN: 978-0-9870198-8-2

THE 2016 WRITIVISM ANTHOLOGY

SUNDOWN

AND OTHER STORIES

Contents

SHORT STORY WINNER

Sundown

Acan Innocent Immaculate

It's AD 2050, and humans are waking up to the reality that scientists have lied to them — the sun is dying and with it a civilisation they have painstakingly built over the course of a hundred and fifty thousand years.

A skinny albino boy, fifteen years old, pulls a T-shirt over his head as he walks out of a cosy bungalow and grins up at the red sky. He's the only human alive who's happy to see the sun on her glorious deathbed; it's a relief to not have to wear hats, sunglasses and long-sleeved shirts any more. The scientists no one trusts say that the sun has a few weeks to go; days even. The boy's scuffed sneakers kick up snow as he makes his way down the stairs from the porch, and he smiles again.

Ten years ago, before the gold of the sun bled out, leaving in its stead a pale red, it would have been a blistering hot day, and any suggestion of the possibility of snow in these parts would have been laughed out of the door and blamed on the many American shows that had taken over African cable television. Now Uganda is experiencing its first winter and one of the greenest countries in the world is now as white as... well, snow.

Inside a large frosted-glass dome, the boy sees the rounded figure of his caretaker, Nyambura. The dome is one of many advanced greenhouses that have popped up all around the world in the past decade as a food source and haven for Earth's nearly depleted plant kingdom. Nyambura moves towards the dome's opening and the boy grimaces, trying to move as quickly as he can towards the gate. It's futile.

"*Red Sun!* Don't you dare walk out of that gate without a jacket and your oxygen tank!" Nyambura shouts.

She is a plump woman, her face shrewd and her skin smoother than one would expect of a 65-year-old woman. Nyambura has been taking care of Red Sun since he was a baby. It is she who, after his parents left in the Mass Exodus, named him Red Sun. She claims that the sun turned red on the exact date of his fifth birthday, but he knows there is more to it; it's a private joke between her and the lanky, one-legged askari who is Kenyan, like her, and laughs every time he hears or says Red Sun's name.

Red Sun finds Nyambura's voice more cutting than the alien cold that permeates the air of Nakasongola. Red returns to the house and re-emerges with a thick sweater on and a blue tank strapped to his back. He slaps the gas mask over his nose and mouth, inhales deeply, for Nyambura's benefit, and returns it to its perch on his shoulder. "Happy now?"

The look on Nyambura's face forebodes another lecture on respect for elders, but she surprises him by crossing the snow-covered compound to hug him. Bemused, he looks down at the colourful scarf covering her greying hair, and a spurt of rage overtakes him.

The people in charge of the Mass Exodus should have taken Nyambura with them on their big exclusive spaceships. It shouldn't have mattered that she was above the age limit they had set, or that she was no genius with perfect genes. She is the perfect embodiment of what the soul of the human race needs: compassion, love and altruism, and expertise in wielding an iron glove when the previous qualities do not yield the desired results.

Of course, to the single-minded scientists, politicians and environmentalists in charge, those weren't the qualities required to be allowed onto their generation ships. When Red was six, the Mass Exodus began. There was only room for half of the world's population, they said. They had to take only the crème de la crème of the race, they said, because it was crucial that when the ships finally stumbled upon a habitable planet, humanity put its best foot forward in the race to propagate and continue itself. So the old, the crippled, the diseased, and the people with genes that had gone haywire ... those would have to be abandoned.

A sacrifice for the greater good of the race as a whole, they said. Red scoffs. He still remembers the day they came for his parents and his sister. Under normal circumstances, his parents would have been left behind — they were both carriers of the albino mutant gene, and that was undesirable in the new world the bureaucrats envisioned. But they were brilliant scientists.

Red's father had been an understudy in his mother's laboratory when, together, they had discovered both a way to extract oxygen from water, and a baser chemistry between each other. The bureaucrats needed their skills. He still remembers the foolish trust in his mother's eyes when the bureaucrats told her they would return for him later.

He stopped waiting when the last ships left the earth. They would be many light years away by the time the sun died; the scientists had ensured that.

"Red..." Nyambura's voice is now gentle, a glaring contrast to the tone she had used before, "you're daydreaming again."

He wants to laugh. Aren't daydreams supposed to be beautiful? He disentangles himself from Nyambura's arms and, this time, makes it to the gate without her stopping him. The askari is seated in his little house at the gate, polishing his metallic leg and whistling a merry tune while the one leg that he can still feel taps a beat on the smooth cement floor.

"Jambo," Red greets in Kiswahili, his head ducked. He hasn't quite overcome his wariness of the askari who, they say, lost his leg in the Third World War after he felled an entire battalion of Congolese soldiers.

The askari grins, baring a set of teeth blackened by years of smoking and, in a hoarse voice, responds in English, "You're going out again, eh? Go and explore, boy. See if you can find a solution to our problems in the barrenness out there."

Red says nothing and continues to walk, the maniacal laugh of the askari following him until he turns the bend that leads to the old man Kazinda's ranch, which used to be full of cows and bulls, but even those have disappeared, taken either by the ravages of hunger or on spaceships that were set apart to carry samples of earth's fauna and flora. Vaguely, Red recalls a rhyme from a Bible story.

The animals went in two by two...

Against his volition, he thinks about the gruesome images from TV when the animals started dying from hunger, the death that climbed up the food chain until all that were left were the vultures and flies that thrived on the dead, and the reptiles and amphibians that thrived on the flies. He closes his eyes for a moment. And after that, the Great Floods had taken care of the animals that had survived. People died too, during the Mass Extinction. The flies carried disease, and people ate the dead animals. The result was that a population of the four billion left behind fell to just a few hundred million.

Snow begins to fall. It does that more often these days. The snow stops falling long enough for the hydrogen-powered winter-service vehicles to shovel it off the roads, and then it starts up again. Red holds out his hands to catch the white crystals. They float gently into his palms and do not melt — his hands are too cold. He used to hate the snow when it first started to fall. Cold, prickly, frozen water, sticking to his skin and making his clothes soggy... He really had hated the snow.

He understands it better now, though. It did not choose to be here; it was forced into this situation by the dying sun. It is just like him. The snow falls with more gusto. Red knows Nyambura will soon send the askari with the snow mobile to come get him. Red breaks into a run. He doesn't want to be found yet.

Nakasongola was a sleepy town before the Mass Exodus. Not small by any means, but sleepy nonetheless, roused only when the flow of traffic was at its peak. Now it is a dead town. Snow blows into the open windows of abandoned shops, and an old Shell signpost peeks through a huge pile of snow. Red has forgotten what the town looks like underneath the carpet of ice. He makes his way towards the large abandoned church he used to go to with his parents and his sister.

The wooden double doors are frozen at the seams, and he has to scrape the ice away with his brittle fingernails, the cold making him oblivious to the possibility of frostbite or injury. Halfway through the meticulous task, he stops to inhale deeply from his oxygen tank. Red goes back to scraping the ice away and hopes that the sun dies before all of the atmospheric oxygen freezes into unbreathable crystals. He would rather cease to exist than live a life that hinges on the insulated metallic tank he hates carrying around.

The wind picks up and blows bits of ice into Red's face. He has always hated the wind, and will continue to do so. It is the snow's bad-tempered older cousin, influencing the crystals of ice to change from gently cool to violently frigid, leaving cuts all over Red's delicate skin.

He finally removes the last of the ice sealing the doors shut and pushes them open, his arms straining and his breath huffing out as his muscles eat up the meagre oxygen available, to counteract the resistance offered up by the rusty hinges.

The inside of the church is warm. The townsfolk claim that it's the spirit of the Christian God who keeps the building that way, but Red knows better. It was built by American evangelists who preferred cheaper building materials – double-wood walls with air pockets to insulate against the cold. They probably had no idea that the Great Freeze was coming, but Red is sure that if they were here today, they would claim that they had seen it in visions from their God, and were instructed to build the church this way.

If they were here right now, they would probably be atheist, like most of rest of the world these days. Another excerpt from the Bible plays in his mind.

Lord, Lord, why have you forsaken me?

It seems to him like it's the other way round: the world has turned its back on the gods it used to worship. Crime is rampant in the bigger cities, where people gather like seals in the Arctic, seeking comfort in the same masses that kill them.

Red likes it in his deserted town, where his closest neighbour lives ten minutes away. His sneakers barely make a sound as he walks down the aisle towards the altar. On either side of him, the brown pews are covered with cobwebs whose makers are now extinct. A small door off to the side of the altar is ajar, and it is through this door that Red walks.

"You're underdressed for the weather."

Red's companion stands with his back to the entrance, wearing a thick overcoat and fur boots two sizes too big. He's shorter than most — his dreadlocked head comes just up to Red's waist, and his hands are invisible in the sleeves of the overcoat he probably nicked from a taller person.

"How can you tell?" Red demands.

The dwarf chuckles. "Your teeth are chattering, and I can smell your wet sneakers."

Red ignores the jibe, walks over to the pile of books on the floor, plops down onto his butt, and picks up a book at random: *Quantum Physics*. These are his mother's books. He carried them here, methodically, day by day, from the sacred library in the house.

A moment later, the dwarf joins him on the floor and picks up a book of his own. They've been meeting here for the past four months, and the dwarf has been helping him understand his parents' art. Nyambura does not approve: she tells Red that dwarves are a bad omen. But she no longer bothers him about his regular visits to the church.

"Let the boy go where he pleases," the askari always tells her. "We are all going to die anyway, one way or another."

Sometimes, Red thinks that Nyambura lets him go exploring so that he doesn't hear the dark words that spring from the askari's heart.

"From the heart," the dwarf always says. "That's where all our words come from. The lies come from the surface and the truths from the deep corners where the light does not reach."

Red isn't sure whether the dwarf is sane or not. He fluctuates with terrifying ease from philosopher to physicist to biologist to linguist to theologian. Every so often, he wanders off with his thoughts, his bleary eyes clearing for that prolonged moment of mental travel, and then he's back on the floor with Red, telling him that the eighteenth-century scientists had it all figured out, and science started to go to hell when these newbies from the twenty-first century began to believe that they were greater than the universe.

Half the time, Red zones out. The thing that holds the most interest for him is the law of conservation of energy. He is fascinated by the idea that nothing ever ceases to exist in reality, that everything is energy that will never be destroyed.

He spends his days with the dwarf poring over writings by Einstein, Galileo, Joule, Leibniz and Noether, attempting to convince his teenage mind that the certainty of his death should not be a thing that concerns him, for he shall continue to live on in another form.

"The end is nigh," the dwarf says suddenly.

Red puts down his book to stare at his formerly silent companion. He recognises the clear, faraway look in the dwarf's eyes. He's having one of his episodes again. Red elects to pay attention to the dwarf's blabbering this time.

"The end is nigh and humanity has brought it upon itself," the dwarf says in an ominous voice.

We'll go out with a bang, Red muses. *Isn't that the only way to go?* Outside, the engine of a snow mobile rumbles. A few seconds later, someone pounds at the door.

The dwarf speaks without looking up from his scribbling: "You should go."

Red gets to his feet without argument. He makes it to the door before the sounds of the dwarf getting up stop him. He turns, and is met by the outstretched hand of his eccentric companion. For a moment, he is stumped. The dwarf has never initiated physical contact. Hesitantly, he takes the proffered hand and shakes.

"The first and last time we shall shake hands," the dwarf says cryptically. His words haunt Red even after he gets home.

*

That night, Red doesn't feel like sleeping alone. The sky is a pale pink, and the moon is a bloody red that wouldn't irk him on any other day, but now makes an old apocalyptic Christian hymn play over and over again in his head.

Oh, when the moon turns into blood...

He climbs out of his parents' bed and walks out of the master bedroom that he has taken over. Three doors down the hallway, he stops and knocks at Nyambura's door. She asks no questions and makes no remonstration; simply makes room for him in her bed and wraps her warm arms around him. In her gentle voice, she hums the lullaby she used to sing him before his parents left. A few seconds later, he is asleep.

*

The heat wakes Red up. It is too intense to be from Nyambura's sleeping form. He throws the blankets back; his body is drenched in sweat and covered in a bright-white light that he realises is spilling in through the windows to flood the entire room. He makes his way out of the bedroom and onto the porch.

Outside, the light nearly blinds him and makes his eyes hurt. It reminds him of the days before the Red Giant phase, when he couldn't step out of the house without layers of clothing and sunglasses.

A burn registers on his exposed skin, and he steps off the porch. His toes curl when his feet hit slush instead of ice packed solid. He slips; his arms flail ineffectually for balance, and he lands on the slush with a splash. The pain in his backside goes unnoticed in the face of the blinding, burning light.

This is it, he thinks.

He half expects the God from Bible stories to descend from the sky, with bronzed feet and a beard and robe as white as the melting snow around him. With considerable effort, he gets to his feet, and immediately a strong invisible wave nearly knocks him back down.

Before he can grasp the implications of the wave, a chasm cracks across the ground right in front of him. Red jumps back with a startled gasp. He watches the chasm rip the house he calls home into two, and terror that was concealed by confusion comes to the forefront.

This is it.

He wants to run into the crumbling house to grab Nyambura, if not to save her, then to throw himself into her embrace and die in the security of her arms, but he can't get himself to move another step.

It has always been his destiny to die with the sun, hasn't it? Of course it has. Red steps towards the chasm. Vaguely, he hears the askari yell for him to stop over the thundering of a million earthquakes. He couldn't stop if he tried to.

One foot makes it into the chasm, and earth's gravity gives, and Red floats into the white sky, together with a billion animate and inanimate objects; he sees the askari in his peripheral vision, his posture a study in befuddlement. Another of the waves crashes through the air. A metallic chair sails languorously past Red's head, and his arms spread out in a sacrificial gesture.

He is ready to die. Perhaps he has always been ready to die. The waves continue to come in quicker succession, and more objects fly past and into Red's prone body, hitting him with all the impact of a feather.

The bright white in the sky is joined by the bright red from the earth's core as it starts to disintegrate. Is it happening too quickly or too slowly? Red can't tell. He is reaching for the infinite space that is just a moment away. He can't breathe. Is there something blocking his nose?

He realises, a second later, that he can in fact breathe, but it's the oxygen. The forces of the universe have denied his unspoken request that the sun die before the oxygen is depleted. Or have they? He can't think clearly now; his brain tissues are feeling the oxygen deprivation. A goofy smile forms on his face. It is goofy; he can tell. The white light is now fading. So is the air. He can't breathe. His lungs are becoming one with the endless vacuum that is space.

One more wave, stronger than the rest, cuts through the sudden blackness. A force pulls on Red. Piece by piece, he's disintegrating just as the earth did. Is this what a black hole feels like? The pain does not matter. He is giving back what was taken from the universe to make him. It's just a cycle.

His final thought is the only thing that escapes the ravenous pull of the dying star, and it is sent out into the vast blackness to float among the stars:

Energy cannot be created or destroyed, but only changed from one form into another or transferred from one object to another.

NON FICTION WINNER

Lost Futures, or A Guide to Losing Love

YKO Tetteh

"The real beauty in life is that beauty can sometimes occur."
Colum McCann, Dancer, 2003

"We tell ourselves stories in order to live." Joan Didion, The
White Album, 1979

There is still time for something to be salvaged.

I make a drastic move, take a chance with a boldness I don't feel, and place myself awkwardly in his lap. His long body could swaddle me up; his legs lift to bring me closer into an enclosure completed by the doughy flesh of his arms.

He has the soft skin of older men. It's textured like chicken skin, but also smooth and sanded, drawing my fingers to it, and my cheek.

He says nothing, keeps his eyes on the game, legs outstretched towards the TV. I bring my elbow to his left shoulder and put my fist to my chin in a gesture uniting boredom and expectation.

"Can I ask you something?"

Hearing my voice is uncomfortable to me. I don't know how to feel so can't regulate it — it's strained slightly, and almost childish. He sighs, lifts his glasses and rubs his eyes with the fingers of one hand. It hurts me, but I need something to happen.

I panic though, in the silence, not knowing how to tell him I'm lingering because I'm waiting for the moment that makes it worth it.

Or how to tell him I'm trying to ignore that the feeling between us is not love. That I do know it. That when I say, "I have love for you," it's because I don't think I have — but I want to. Though I can't say why.

I don't know how to say these things, but we both know another reckoning is inescapable, so I grasp at something, start somewhere:

"Will you think of me when I'm gone?" I ask.

"Why would you ask that? What do you want?" He lifts me off his lap, leaves the room, returns. "I honestly don't know if I will. That's just the kind of person I am." The words come out forcefully, determined rather than attacking. "I can't predict these things. I've tried to be honest with you about who I am. I just don't know, and I just can't feel bad about these things any more."

He had told me. He'd told me he was "stuck." I knew he had four "elite" academic degrees, and little sense of himself. I knew he was depressed. I knew he was jobless and without hope. And that I was young and dreamy and ambitious — in love as much as in life.

He talks, I talk. We hug, and he walks me to the subway station. On the track I think about the quiet, pulsating sadness in me. I'm tempted to ask, "How did I get here?" But I resist, because I know how I got here: I grew up on a potent mix of fantasy novels and anime. On infinite afternoons spent soul-deep in stories that were both epic — and reassuringly predictable. On hours sat swallowing into myself thousands of pages of love stories, journeys and supernatural worlds saturated with meaning. On a bread and butter of crucial quests: for selfhood, and for love. Which is to say I grew into fantastic and deeply compelling (and disastrous) ideas about love, and into a long-enduring faith in the triumph of the human spirit.

I wasn't even nerdy, or particularly withdrawn. I didn't have a bad childhood. I had a large garden, and went to private school, and won all the races on Sports Day. Yet there was something that drew me endlessly into the refuge of lives that were not my own, lives of Protagonists with Great Purpose – and that made sense.

That's something: my life didn't make all that much sense. And because we don't talk about things in my family, I was left to decipher nonsensical happenings alone in my youthful head.

Things like being a British-born Ghanaian girl in post-apartheid South Africa, and being woefully unqualified to decide how to interact with the black housekeepers in my white friends' houses. Things like my father being in my life only sporadically from when I was four till twelve years old; years he spent mostly as a weekend visitor, or the invisible subject of my mother's sneering comments, or an occasional voice on the phone. After which he became an unspoken absence — and that has not changed.

And other nonsensical things like my mother's love. Unfailing, and punishing; the intense love of single mothers who've had to make it work, for years, by themselves. The kind of love that has had to burn relentlessly against hard times and loneliness, so it needs your love for fuel. Sometimes beyond what you might be ready to give.

In this kind of nonsensical world you need cohering life-narratives like, "We have it together; we are a family." But, unlike the extensively woven narratives I read, these ones were fragile. Such unwieldy, disruptive things as emotions could never be felt on the surface — only secretly.

So it was on the powerful tides of all those many epic fantasies that I learnt there is an ocean of feeling. That there are capital-C characters whose emotional strength is so great it moulds destinies beyond even their own lives. In every one of these emotional movements, in every awakening of hidden magical power, I learnt what it is to feel. And for those feelings to be felt so completely they manifest outside of you in rolling balls of energy.

You can feel everything in these stories.

And that's how I grew up — feeling everything in stories.

Sometimes I narrate my life to myself; matching my narration style to whichever author I happen to be reading. I'll move my mouth around words over and over again until they resonate with some deeply felt truth I'd struggle to define. Sometimes the stories move beyond my body and draw into themselves the stories I've read. To help me, I think, escape or keep calm.

Like the time my mother stood sobbing in my room, crying that I didn't talk to her — that I didn't love her — and how I tried not to cry. "And instead shut her eyes and felt the broiling force of her emotions so intensely they burst her skin and escaped her control as a wild, untamed magic."

I've been worried many times that I'm crazy. I worry now and I worried when I was eleven, and fantasising frequently about a reincarnated Xena Warrior Princess. The mythic lesbian heroine always appeared, with a dazed and darting expression, in the parking lot of a London council estate. And I appeared, shocked but cognisant, from the door to my uncle's ground-floor council flat. In each iteration I changed some small detail: the words I said, the size of the steps I took, how quickly she came to trust me. Even then I knew it was not make-believe — it was preparation. Anything could happen, and I wanted to be ready.

When Fantasy is your mother's milk, such things are as much unremarkable — commonplace, even — as they are worrying. To believe the churning monotony of your life can be broken by a sudden and wondrous apparition is the natural movement of the mind. An attitude of belief is its natural state. Which is possibly how my well-stocked imagination came to believe in the shifting, formless thing that was the relationship between him and me.

How I came to be sitting in the same coffee shop, watching for the same man, holding the same yearning desires.

"Hey, how are you?" He always exhales this. A short, sharp breath for the greeting, a longer for the question.

He shifts off his backpack, sits next to me on the bench in the wall. I hold myself away from him, imperceptibly, but willing him to note my resistance.

"I'm well, thanks." I smile, taking in the cafe's warm, shadowy light, and its small made-for-one tables, before moving my eyes to meet his face.

I almost move my hand to his when he laughs in the middle of our conversation. His lips pull back and he shows his top teeth, giggling in more short exhales. His boyish face looks lit and even more youthful. I'm buoyed and grateful, and realise I was sinking in the swirl of my thoughts and half-aborted feelings. I want more.

But more is not forthcoming. A man having trouble loving himself cannot love me. So I let us talk about food and editing software and how cold it is in New York City. I don't press him about how he's doing, or whether he's found work, or whether he feels hope. His answers rarely soothe me anyway, and to question would be to belie my longing for him to be well, and grown, and loving finally.

In the books, man-boys (lost, weak and slightly dull) go through trials (they are orphaned, or their village is ransacked; they are often poor). But then they emerge as men (cripplingly beautiful, mature, brave, rich). In real life the outcome is far less certain. But hope is birthed in that uncertainty — and dies hard. So that these flailing man-boys of our physical reality, lost on their way to manhood, are always, in some way, utterly absorbing. And, as the flesh-and-blood extensions of the stories that have nourished us, they cannot be fully dismissed.

In their state of empathy-inducing powerlessness, our living forest rangers inspire all the love and faith and support we have given to their fictional counterparts. Their need compels, such that helping them progress in their journey feels like we're progressing in our own. Feels like we are creating meaning in both our lives, so that experiencing their life becomes an important part of ours. Or, put another way, our narrative needs to be an important part of theirs.

As Laurie Penny, writing on Manic Pixie Dream Girls (MPDG) and sexism in stories, puts it:

> *If we want anything interesting at all to happen to us we have to be a story that happens to somebody else, and when you're a young girl*

looking for a script, there are a limited selection of roles to choose from.

If attaching your life to that of someone who doesn't love you is a special type of madness, the literary phenomenon of the MPDG is the closest I've come to a diagnosis. The Manic Pixie Dream Girl term, Penny explains, was coined first by Nathan Rabin. He described her as existing "solely in the fevered imaginations of sensitive writer-directors to teach broodingly soulful young men to embrace life and its infinite mysteries and adventures."

Reading this for the first time was deliciously satisfying; it was familiar. Moulding my narrative to that of "broodingly soulful" men had become, by the time I reached the doctor's office of Laurie Penny MPDG, a chronic condition.

I had already, in the twenty-three years of my life, devotedly sought to nurture intimacy and hope in that of a disillusioned and penniless PhD. I had also, and to much chagrin, dated a "misunderstood", roguishly beautiful, Jack Sparrow-esque homeless man in Hawaii. And I had certainly — and frequently — heard myself explain in long, circling monologues that such-and-such love interest "just needed time" and "a little help" to be in touch with their feelings. (A necessary precursor to transforming into the loving, thoughtful partner I so desire.)

This disease of Manic Pixie-ness is deeply unflattering, and worrying, but also wonderful. It makes things make sense. "There's a reason why I act this way!" I can cry. I can clutch this information to myself and explain, "I'm not the only one who does this; it's not just me!"

But also, it's not me.

There's something that's never quite fit: I'm black. And neither in the books nor in the many (many) dreamscapes of whimsy-seeking men are Manic Pixies black. Or of any colour. No, they are cute waifs with sparkling eyes; fragile, yoghurty skin; and delicate bodies.

I should have remembered that we black women have already been assigned our narratives — and they are not the type to inspire affection in the hearts of sensitive men. Our narratives — the ones largely designated by men wanting to map their thoughts onto our bodies — are of a different calibre. We're not excitable, endearingly strange, sensitive or cute. We are "strong" and "athletic" and, of course, "exotic". Thank you for the compliments, Mr [white] Man.

In the market of romantic exchange, your narrative affords (and robs) you certain allowances and rewards. Manic Pixie Dream Girls are robbed of a full personality, of strength and of agency — but they get the hearts of sweet, deep-thinking boy-men and soft-boys. Not really a win, but such is love. Strong black women with thighs and thoughts get to have power. Or whatever you might call that intimidating veneer to our persons. What we don't get are emotions. Or that lovely ethereal quality. We are, indeed, some of the most solid-form human beings you will meet, and we are meant never to waiver; we may be enticing, but never ungraspable.

How we are grasped, as has been the fate of women of our gender, is not up to us. And if how we are grasped is our social currency, then how worrying to feel my actions have no apparent sense or structure — no obvious narrative. I do not fit into either of the categories — or rather, I fit into both. I exhibit the core MPDG behaviours ("Here suffering man, let me help you"), yes. But my actions, without the context of the MPDG body, situated in a strong, black and dependable woman's body, are even more absurd. I am rendered just a person making inexplicable decisions. And inexplicable decisions often look like stupid decisions.

Like dating a man who prefers solitude to intimacy and does not subscribe to holding hands. A melancholy, tired man, in every single way unsuitable for a dreamy, physical young woman with precisely enough verve to stay in a lifeless relationship for two years. It's not that I haven't known; I know you're not supposed to be afraid all the time of the unpredictable moment. The one that topples the good feeling you work so hard to construct in the short time things are going well.

I suppose I've been waiting, I imagine, just as I waited for dozens of storied heroes before him, for this male protagonist to come into his best self. And for our relationship to evolve along with him. I've been holding, most importantly, onto the hope of such a future.

The hope that I could have something approximating love in something approximating a relationship with someone approximating a mature emotionally developed partner. The hope that I could grow into love with someone. That hope, to a love-naïve, fantasy-reared, dreamy-but-solid young black woman, feels crucial.

If I let him go and rid myself of those alien-seeming manic pixie dream girl tendencies, if I gave up on him and gave into realism, if I abandoned the fantasy of an improbable love — what would be the collateral damage?

I know what I would gain: comprehensibility. Often called by another name: maturity.

I think of this whenever I remember the drive to Honolulu. I'm not with him; I'm with a friend. In the car I put my feet up on the dashboard, stick my right foot out the window, and curl my toes in the passing wind.

"I have to say, Y—, I think that's pretty immature of you."

I sit up and bring my feet down. "What makes you say that?"

"I just feel like it's sort of immature that you want to be with this guy just because you want to be the girl that 'reaches' him. He's pretty weird."

I start talking.

Pushing out words I already know are failing to make him understand. But I continue, hands moving in useless gestures alongside my voice, because I don't want to believe I'm defenceless against the settling weight of his judgment. I don't want to be left alone with the fury of being reduced to such a damning flaw. Or with the hurt of being misunderstood. What seems simple to him seems impossibly complicated to me: why don't I just... not?

So I should be relieved, sitting a continent away in the lounge of my uncle's house, when I get the text from the man.

"Hey Y——. I have crazy news. I got married last week. Everything happened really quickly for various reasons. We actually only started seeing each other in the Fall and even then, tentatively. It's crazy and strange, especially for me, but I was stuck in every way and my life had to change and so I let it. It's been a hard thing to figure out how to share with you. Maybe we'll get a chance to talk about it sometime."

I move to another room. Clutching my phone, I scramble to exorcise myself of all the hopes at love I had invested in him. I want to be rid of him, and quickly. And to be rid of that extra thing: the sharp, suddenly inescapable feeling that there will be many other people I will never love.

I feel the loss of him (and the others) keenly and abruptly, right in the spot between the bottom of my ribs and my belly button. I wonder if I should cry. I hope I do, and instead feel the pressure of a silence of emotion. I consider cancelling my drinks date with a local artist, but recognise, disconcertingly, that I'm composed enough to go. Instead, my hands move and my feelings grasp at anger. I delete the text and block the contact. His punishment is never to hear from me again.

"Uncle, I'm headed out!"

But there's an aching residue of something that feels like sorrow. It's in my chest and my throat, and it makes me clench my fingers. Would that I could scour myself of this feeling. Perhaps this is precisely the time to do as people have been calling for me to do: exorcise myself not of other people, but of that irrational, compulsive part of me that pursues poor prospects. Life would probably be easier. Perhaps I should try to find a way. Perhaps those same people calling for change could also tell me whom I would be left to be?

I grew myself up on stories and feelings.

If the risk of getting hurt goes, if the "bad" decisions and inappropriate men and incomprehensible impulses go, then so do my daring and positivity. So goes my dogged belief in the triumph of the human spirit – and in love. The imagination that has me believing in futures where love is mature (and so are the men) is the same imagination that envisioned what life might be like in other worlds and in other bodies. It is the basis of my empathy. It is the basis of my hope.

Which is what continues to be so disturbing about the text from the man I had hoped to love, who got married. His moving on — so drastically and so swiftly — undermined my imagination and my dreams. I felt him close a door and leave me with a cold new hardness to the undulating, dreamy way I feel through life. Things end.

I've learnt a lesson; I'm cautious. I've said flippantly and spitefully "all men are liars". I subscribe to the belief that straight cis men are the worst demographic. I am hurt. I accept the painful but mundane reality that I am not special. I am not exempt from loss. I am not special.

Which would be harder to swallow if not for the stories that got me here in the first place. I suppose a by-product of a near-constant and multiplatform consumption of narratives about Awesome Beings will fast-forward the realisation that you are, by most measures, unremarkably average.

Which is precisely why you live and feel in stories to begin with. Yes, fine, the misery of your own mundanity is painful, but at least you also have dreams. I say that even now. In the midst of the pain (any pain), hope and triumph and love become these tenacious and elemental forces — sources upon which you draw in the process of creating your narrative. One replete with Significant Moments and a sense that you might just be, or at least experience, something more.

It's actually pretty... hopeful.

SHORT FICTION
SHORTLIST

Boyi

Gloria Mwaniga

Madness entered Mama's eyes the day Baba pushed my brother, Boyi, towards Matwa Kei and said to him, "Hold on to the boy until I find your 40,000 land protection tax, and then I will have him back."

After Baba had put the latch on the door inside and Boyi and the men had been swallowed by the darkness outside, Mama stood up as though fire ants had invaded her body. She tore off her *kitenge* headscarf and started to shout. She told Baba he was sick in the head to think Boyi would return. Was he deaf? Had his ear not caught stories of neighbours' sons who had been recruited by the SALADEF Militia? Did he think a child was like a mat that a person folded and gave back to the owner after sitting on, or a dress, which one could borrow from a neighbour?

Baba just sat there and held his rage firmly with his hands. He pulled in his lips to a narrow thread, like a line drawn on his dark face by a ruler. His voice then sank to a metallic whisper and he asked Mama what she wanted him to do. Didn't she know that they chopped off the heads of whole families if you didn't give them money? Hadn't she heard of how they carried off fresh heads like trophies and hung them on trees and maybe even ate them like Idi Amin had? Was she ready for the torture afflicted: first, the slow chopping off of ears and then the feeding of worm-filled earth to the victims?

By the time Baba was finished, hives had broken out on Mama's skin and her eyes were a deathly white, like the eyes of one who did not know her own mind.

I stood at the kitchen door feeling queasy, as if someone had pulled my insides out through my nostrils.

*

We had known that they would come to our house. We knew it the day Baba's friend Chesober, who taught at Chepkurkur Primary School, carried the story to our ears that SALADEF had a long list of people who had aided the government exercise of dividing our land and giving some of it to the Ndorobo.

We knew they would come because Baba had lent a *panga* and *makonge* ropes to the government surveyors that day. So, when the news broke that they had begun attacking government representatives, Mama started blocking the sitting-room door with sacks of maize and beans.

I do not know if it was fear or denial that made Boyi and me laugh at the thought of SALADEF attacking us, their Soy tribe mates. I only know that we were laughing about it the night Matwa Kei knocked on our door and told Baba, "Mzee, give us the 10,000 land protection tax and 30,000 betrayal tax or today we will show you smoke without fire."

Baba brought out everything he owned. His savings which had lain hidden in a metal box under his bed. His precious Sony transistor radio. Even his hunting gun. In the end, desperate to save his family, he promised to sell our bull Mtambakaki the next day and give SALADEF all the cash.

Matwa Kei simply shook his head and said, "You did not wait until tomorrow to lend the *saveya* your *panga* and *makonge*. I will not wait until tomorrow to get the money. Bring it now-now or your whole family is finished today."

That is the moment Baba had pushed Boyi forward and told Matwa Kei to hold on to him. That is the day Baba shook his head sadly and muttered, "Our very boys, who ate oaths to protect our ancestral land, have turned on us like the hungry chameleon that eats its intestines."

*

The morning after Boyi went, I awoke to find Mama sitting on the *kitimoto* in the kitchen. She didn't look up. When I said *vuchee*, she did not reply. And when I made tea and started to pour it into a melamine cup, she shrieked, "Stupid girl, you want to finish tea and your brother will come from the caves hungry. Leave him some."

She screamed over many meals in the weeks that followed. At first I tried to explain to her that Boyi wasn't coming yet and if he came, I would cook him another meal. She only said, "Stupid girl, leave your brother some."

Baba would say, "Shut up, *chesheet*. You will kill Boyi with your torn mouth. He is not dead. You hear me, eeh."

As Baba spoke, Mama would turn her gaze slowly towards the whitewashed wall and in a quiet voice declare that she was seeing a vision of a dazzling white dove. The God of Israel was showing her that my brother had escaped SALADEF and was on his way home.

After her monologues, silence would sit in the room like a fourth person.

*

Many of the neighbours visited us after Boyi went. They came to shake their heads and say, "I stand with you." Others shrugged, asked if there was anything they could do. Still, others came to give us stories about people who had disappeared and then miraculously come back. Sometimes, if Mama's madness had taken a walk and she looked better, we would brew tea together and then she would sit with the visitors and tell stories about Boyi. How Boyi saved her marriage by confirming that her womb wasn't tied up by Djinnis. How Boyi's ebony skin had a particular naked smoothness like the bark of a guava tree. How Boyi spoke excellent English, English that was too good for a fifteen year old like him.

I used to leave the kitchen door slightly open for the clink of tea cups and the voices to reach my ears.

After some time, however, the stream of visitors became a trickle and then we would stay a whole day without anyone coming to drink tea and to say *anyoogaat*.

*

A full moon was rising outside the night Saulo carried the story to us wrapped in his spittle-moist lips. I saw his bald head over the bougainvillea fence and rushed to open the door.

"The government has decided to put its head into the matter by launching Operation Okoa Maisha," he said. "A troop of two hundred Kenya Armed Forces men have already been dispatched in huge green lorries. They are coming to flush out the SALADEF. The land war has gone on too long and it is us, *us*, who have forced the mighty arm of the government." He spat out the words "mighty arm" like over-chewed sugarcane pith and swung his thick arm in the air.

*

Early next morning, Baba and his cousin Kimutai dug a shallow grave at the back of the house and buried a banana stem wrapped in a green cotton sheet.

"Death, take this body," Baba muttered. "Take it and do not bother my home with your visits again."

I stood near the pit watching and wondering why Baba, a Christian, could believe such things. The organic scent of moist earth made my eyes water. I did not look at Mama, who sat on the soggy ground next to me tightly hugging the *kikoyi* written "*amani haipatikani ila kwa ncha ya upanga*; peace cannot be found by the edge of the machete."

Mama refused to throw fresh soil on the grave and only followed Baba's movements with her eyes as he shovelled lumps onto the grave. When he had put a wooden cross on the mound of fresh earth, Mama said, with a manic vibrancy in her voice, that she would not participate in escorting Boyi's spirit away.

*

The long rains came and fell with both hands.

The water gouged out deep channels and swept away twigs, leaves and top, fertile soil from the *shamba*. Chocolate-coloured rivulets collected into a single rapid that flowed down onto the main road and collected on both sides. The mountain wind blew hard. It snapped the tap roots of young maize crops, tore them out of the earth so that they lay like dead green snakes. Windows rattled, doors slammed against houses and leaves fluttered up like lost kites.

The mountain wind also yanked off the tin roof of our mud-and-wattle kitchen. It wrenched it off the day I smelt for the first time a sickly-sweet bloody whiff from the Elgon forest. The scent rose like a gigantic bird and hovered higher and higher, finally enfolding houses and *shambas* in the spread of its phantom wings.

It was also the day the jungle-green Kenya Army lorries arrived.

All of us children ran through the light afternoon drizzle and stood shoulder to shoulder at the roadside to watch the convoy. We prayed the lorries would get stuck in mud so we could peek at the soldiers' cobra-skin belts, which we had been told sucked away pot bellies. The men joined us so that we lined up the main road like vertical dashes, waving madly at the soldiers with inverted green bowls on their heads.

The womenfolk abandoned their pots and water vessels and clambered up to the road to join us in trading stories about the army's expensive colognes, which smelt of pork to scare off dead spirits. Someone started a tale about the soldiers' hippo-leather boots, which made their feet smooth like the buttocks of new-born babies.

*

In the days that followed, Mama stopped touching her food and started muttering to herself. Her *ugali* would remain untouched until a crusty brown film formed and I had to throw it away in the chicken coop. I used to sit at the kitchen steps so that she was within my line of vision and I'd catch the twist of her mouth as she engaged in the monologues.

"Have I not suffered enough? Have I not? God, tie a rope around my stomach." Sometimes, she'd look up, notice me and say, "*Lakwetaap baai*, do you remember? Do you remember Boyi's perfect teeth, eeh?" She'd go on and on, croaking out the same old question over and over like an accordion, cutting me short whenever I attempted to answer.

After weeks of watching Mama, I got tired and started going with the rest of the children to the chief's camp in Cheptap-burbur, where the army had pitched their green tents. At the armoury, we spent hours peeping through the cypress fence. We eavesdropped on the soldiers' conversations and then made up fabulous tales from them.

"Do you know that very black officer they call *Sah-gent?* Imagine he is the one who defeated Idi Amin in Uganda. I heard him tell the others that Matwa Kei has more magic than Amin even, *wallahi*, that man is a real djinni."

I'd picture Matwa Kei's favourite Chicago Bulls red cap absorbing Sah-gent's booming bullets so that they didn't burst his puffy red eyes.

The stories bubbled like pots of boiling soup. They made me think of the tales Boyi used to tell me about SALADEF: How they drank magic potions from *Orkoiyot* so that their bodies, like the Luo legend Lwanda Magere, would become stone and the enemy's spears would slide off them. How SALADEF's bodies were embalmed in bloody cow dung to make them invisible so that their raiding missions were always successful. How when SALADEF marched through dry land, clouds of red dust would rise up to the heavens like a swarm of locusts because the earth god *Yeyiin* went with them.

I held on to these stories tightly. Willing them to be true.

Willing Boyi to be more powerful than the soldiers.

*

I remember that December like it was yesterday. The farmers didn't clear their *shambas* for the second planting of the maize crop because SALADEF stole young crops from the fields and goats from the pens. Instead of working, the womenfolk stayed at home while the men gathered in little groups under *mtaragwa* trees and exchanged news about how SALADEF cut up people and threw the bloodied bodies in rivers, pit latrines and public wells.

I heard our neighbour, Koros, tell Baba one day: "They now go from house to house forcefully recruiting boys as young as ten. Who knows what their mission is any more? They have forgotten that they were to protect our land from being given to those lazy Ndorobos. Now, they even cut off our necks. After all, isn't Soy blood red like Ndorobo blood? I hear the recruited have to first go back home and kill a close relative so that their hearts are strong to kill others."

"Ndugu Koros," Baba had replied solemnly, "this thing should have ended a long time ago, but *puoot*, war is a maggot that nibbles and nibbles at the hearts of men."

That night I dreamt that Boyi, whose eyes were the same colour as Coca-Cola, came and cut me into small-small pieces so that his heart would become strong to kill. I woke up feeling like an anchorless red balloon was floating in my stomach.

*

The mass exodus to Bungoma and Uganda began the day my breasts became painful, stone-hard lumps in my chest. My friend Chemutai, before her family moved away to Chwele, said that my breasts grew too fast because I spent too much time lying on the ground outside the *musasa* tree reading books instead of working *chap-chap* like a normal girl.

The villages of Kopsiro, Saromet, Chepyuk and Chelebei all had a thick yellow fog of fear over them. The fear came because nobody understood the mind of SALADEF any more. We talked about how the militia now took away young girls to go and cook for them. One lady said she knew a woman who, because she had sent away all her sons, was ordered by Matwa Kei to give him her daughter to go and cook for SALADEF.

There were other stories as well. Darker tales. Stories of how River Cheptap-burbur was scarlet with fresh blood from the human heads floating in. Stories of how the militia raped their own blood relatives who ended up giving birth to babies transparent as plastic bags. When the stories reached our house, Mama said she would never run away and leave Boyi and if Baba wanted to go, he could go and leave her with her tears. Mama, who had always sided with Baba.

Because nobody went to school any more, I spent my days under the Nandi flame tree with half-closed eyes. I imagined Boyi's plastic-bag baby playing *Tinker-tailor-soldier-sailor* with boats that fell from the flame tree.

*

The news came with the dust devil that whirls in January. The very wind that yanked my silk skirt from where I had tucked it between my legs — lifting it up, up above my waist like an upside-down umbrella. Perhaps it was Mama's mourning that had courted misfortune. Maybe even it was Baba's total refusal to talk about Boyi that made our ancestors forget to protect him.

It had been raining, so I was standing at the kitchen window staring at the little silver droplets that shone like handfuls of glittering rice being poured from the sky when I saw Chesaina. An old friend of Baba, he worked as a watchman in a grain depot in faraway Chwele market. I was therefore surprised to see him visit. He sat on the animal-print sofa, then told Mama and Baba that he had got word from a Bukusu trader, who got it from the mouth of a big government man, that Boyi was now a marked man.

"He is Matwa Kei's right-hand man, imagine. My God, Mama Boyi, this war has taken with it the mind of your son."

I hid behind the kitchen door watching Mama with the tail of my eye.

"No!" she hissed in her old voice. "I must not be told me such rubbish about my son. Chesaina, if you want Omo to wash your dirty mouth, just say so." Her eyes flooded with tears and she put both hands on her head. "Matwa Kei, what did I ever do to you? Tell me, Matwa Kei, tell me now so that I can repent."

Her voice choked and I wanted to say, "Chesaina, shut up," but my tongue was clammy and it stuck to the roof of my mouth. Baba tried to calm Mama. He told her that Boyi was a good son and did she remember how he used to recite the responsorial psalm so earnestly, with tears in his eyes? Mama kept crying and so Chesaina walked out in the rain. That day, I saw Baba's tears: two silver streams rolling down polished porcelain.

*

That night I slept on Boyi's bed for the first time.

His blue bed sheets, with prints of chicks coming out of yellow eggshells, enfolded me with a deathly coolness. They smelt so much like him; of his boyish laughter that shone like toffees wrapped in silver foil, of brown butterscotch sweets that appeared as if by magic from his sticky pockets. I remembered how he used to hoard items that Baba had declared illegal — jawbreakers and sticks of Big G that we later stuck under the table. I pressed my sore stone-breasts against the sheets, willing the pain my brother felt in the cold caves onto myself. I imagined him staring with shiny eyes as I told him about the solders, especially *Sah-gent*, whose adventures I knew Boyi would like the most. I imagined us playing Ninja soldier as we had as children, with him wearing his checkered school shirt and me a T-shirt and hiding when he shouted, "Cover, Ninja soldier." Mother had caught us playing that game once and had scolded us for courting misfortune and calling death by name.

*

I knew it was a bad omen the night thunder struck and a bolt of lightning shattered the huge Nandi flame tree at the front of the house. I knew it was a bad omen even though Mama came out of her room and jubilantly declared that the evil that was to come to our house had been struck down and swallowed by the Nandi flame. She then sat next to me on the animal-print sofa and listened to the *tatatata* as the splinters of tree fell on the *mabati* roof and shook the whole house. The Nandi flame tree no longer scattered its embers of blossom upon the earth after that night.

Early the next morning, Simoni dashed into our compound and handed me a copy of the Nation newspaper with the headline "Sabaot Land Defence (SALADEF) Ragtag Militia Leaders Killed by Kenya Army Forces". Everything inside me held. Something throbbed with both fists at my chest as I ran like a mad woman and banged on my parents' bedroom door until Baba shouted, "Do you think the plague of deafness descended on us in the night?"

I didn't stir when Baba finished reading the article and crumpled to the floor like an old coat. I didn't frown when Mama's ribbon laughter pierced the early dawn. I didn't weep when, a few hours later, neighbours started streaming into our house heaving their chests and saying, "It is a bad death that kills a man in the prime of his youth."

Mama didn't roll on the ground when Simoni described how Boyi had been captured deep in the sacred caves. She didn't weep when he said Boyi had been hoisted to the aircraft and then, after it had ascended like a kite, been shoved out by *Sah-gent*.

Mama didn't slap-slap Boyi's corpse asking him why he fed her the bread of sorrow because there was no corpse to slap. Instead, she turned to Baba and looked at him with unclouded, innocent eyes of lunacy. Then with death in her voice she told him that the government *Sah-gent* had thrown her Boyi down "without a parachute, imagine!"

Her voice was not bitter. It was not sad. It was flat. It cracked a little, like dried firewood when fire ate it. Mama didn't fling words at Baba afterwards when he took his Sony transistor radio and the Nation newspaper and threw them into the almost-full pit latrine outside. She didn't say, "If you want to go, go, but leave me alone to mourn with my tears" when I took her hand and led her to Boyi's room. She just sat on the blue bed sheets with prints of chicks coming out of yellow eggshells and spoke Boyi's name softly as though the syllables were made of tin and would hurt the roof of her mouth if she spoke too loudly.

I let the tears roll down my face. I let them soak my blue-silk blouse and purple boob top.

I didn't tell Mama what I knew. I didn't tell her that I had felt life leave Boyi's body. That I had felt it because at the very moment, when the Nandi flame had splintered and shattered, the wind had lost its magic and had turned into an ordinary country wind.

I Haven't Returned

Laure Gnagbe Bledou

Translated from French, *Je ne suis pas rentrée,*

by Edwige-Renée Dro

Pointing towards the imposing white cabinet, Stéphanie calls out to the waitress.

"Madam, excuse me, could you turn it down a bit?"

Sigh of the waitress. Pointed look of Stéphanie. A battle between four dark eyes. Here, Stéphanie has learned that the customer isn't always right. As a friend once told her, "Come on! Think like the sales assistants or the waiters. From their standpoint, it is thanks to them that the business works. Ah yes, seeing that the boss needs them, and the customer as well!

Thankfully, swift victory that evening. No wahala. The waitress grabs the remote control and presses twice on a button. She is generous. With every bip that she hears, Stéphanie knows that she is earning a degree. With a bit of luck, it will be 17 or 18 in a few minutes and they will be able to order.

For Stéphanie, the air con is always too much. In this restaurant, as well as in the shopping centres, the waiting room at the dentist, or in her office. Her colleagues constantly tease that Stéphanie only likes natural cold.

You just have to laugh. Isn't it funny that it feels like you've stepped inside a fridge in Côte d'Ivoire? "In Africa", as her many friends and acquaintances in Europe refer to it.

With time, Stéphanie had learned to just accept some things in each of her environments: the tightly packed Métro in Paris and the dog shit, the lack of pavements in Abidjan and the use of toothpicks at the end of meals (in public); sausages for breakfast in London.

But this way of talking about Africa as if it were a country, she has never been able to accept. Hearing "she lives in Africa", makes her see red. Almost on the edge of violence. How to behave when it is loved ones the culprits? Explain. Explain. Explain.

"If *you* have a friend who lives in Italy, you don't introduce him by saying that he lives in Europe, right? And you don't go on to tell him that you love his country because you've been to Sweden, and you don't also add that you love Paella. Right? Do you then get why I get pissed off?"

"Thank you. That's kind." Stéphanie gives her her most beautiful smile.

The waitress smiles reluctantly, as if she's been thrown off course by the fact that this *métisse* spoiled by life (well-built, light-skinned, with a designer handbag and one who looks like she has her own car) does not play at being boss lady. Stéphanie will give her a tip. No, not because the waitress has done her job by turning down the air con, but to encourage her to do it again … for her, if she ever comes back. It is one of the things Stéphanie has learned in Côte d'Ivoire: more than a thanks, a tip could be an investment. It wasn't always given to reward the quality of the service given, but to buy a future better service. Without forgetting that she heard that in Paris disgruntled waiters could take their revenge by spitting in your dish.

*

Six years since she'd crossed over.

Ever since her first year in High School, which had been one of her best years of African dance lessons, Stéphanie had had everything mapped out. After her baccalaureate, which she passed with honours, followed by two intense years of *Prépa*, she'd got a place at the business school on which she'd set her sights. It had been a sure thing that the module on *Geopolitics of countries in the southern hemisphere* would help her in bringing her project to pass. A project that wasn't only a professional one, but also a life project. A project which she could actually qualify as vital.

During the job interview for a position of project manager in an E-commerce business — a business based in Paris to operate on the African continent, it is more practical like that! — the HR manager had asked her about that module. She hadn't been fooled. It had also been a politically correct way of getting her talking about her "origins". She'd brought out the spiel regarding her two cultures, and of course, had bragged about her ability to adapt. Out of more than ten candidates, she'd been chosen for the role. Determined, disciplined and enthusiastic — three characteristics that are also mentioned in her LinkedIn profile — she'd been promoted in less than six months. The following year, she got transferred, not an expatriation, and as such, none of the advantages that went with it.

That is how Stéphanie came to be back in Abidjan. Sporty and a fashion-lover, she quickly got herself a group of girlfriends just as fun, single and nappy as her. Some had got married (some had clearly settled as far as Stéphanie was concerned) and the same ones (in spite of the image they wanted to portray with their activism for natural hair) had made sure to wait for Step 1 before going onto Step 2; that of having children. Anyway, they'd gone ahead and succeeded, as far as the society in which Stéphanie was living was concerned. Not her.

"What of your husband? Where is your husband?"

The only person whom she accepted those questions from, was her grandma.

Augustine Ouaflé KRANGBO, A.K.A Tchoutchou, born around

January 01st, 1939 on a farm in the west of the country was a tiny woman, who fought hard to make her way in life from birth to managing a little kiosk in Abidjan. From what Stéphanie gathered , no-one or nothing had been able to stand up to the will of her grandmother in 63 years. On this point, Stéphanie was adamant. Her grandmother deserved more than the often consensual and common "Mamie", but instead an appellation deserving of an official title. Keeping in with that, Stéphanie had taken it upon herself to give the titles of "uncle" or "auntie" to some uncles and aunts. That thing of calling every grown-up uncle or auntie had, for a long time, exasperated her. She'd had to bow down to it though even if sometimes, she used her French culture, a culture that was so often mentioned to her (so often …) to free herself up from those kinds of rules.

Unlike the other members of her family, Grandma was not insistent on Stéphanie marrying someone from a good family, or someone, who dressed well. For her granddaughter, she just wanted a life partner, so that she didn't end up alone, like her. Stéphanie was sure of that. She'd understood that one day as she looked into Augustine's eyes, who, not being fluent in French, could not express everything in a language that both understood.

"My child, get married."

"Ah, Grandma, let me first find a man!"

Grandma always looked her straight in the eye, as if waiting for Stéphanie to tell her why she had trouble finding that man, before pouting.

"But you need to hurry up and find him. Me, I need to look after your children before I die."

The way in which she said that always made Stéphanie forget her sadness. According to her girlfriends who'd settled down, finding a nanny in Abidjan was a real headache, but here she was with a ready-made one on her hands. A nanny who was just as motivated as she was impatient!

"Alright, Grandma, I will prioritise that ..."

At that point, Grandma always interrupts her with a correction of her Anglicism and her lack of discernment. (It is a fact that 'will' has nothing to do with finding love).

"My child, I'll pray about it."

"Thanks, grandma. But stop talking about your death. OK?"

"Ahi, but all of us, we are all gonna die hein."

Grandma always had the last word, and that, in five or six languages. Through language trips, an end-of-year internship in Britain and a rigorous discipline (a monthly reading of a book in English, TV series), Stéphanie had passably become fluent in English. All good, but that's all. Unlike Grandma, who, at the school of life, had been able to master Bakoué, Bété, Baoulé, Dioula, and French especially, but that had been to better understand the priest, because with this granddaughter whom she got to know late, the language of the eyes were often enough.

Stéphanie met up with Grandma and her relentless worry for her matrimonial situation once a month, just about. Thankfully, the questions were not too insistent because, to be truthful, Stéphanie's visits were quite short because time was needed to enquire of everyone else's news, then give one's own news.

Stéphanie had instituted this ritual of monthly visits, like the many other rituals she had. It was her thing. Her way of life, even. Stéphanie has to establish syncretic traditions to establish her relations with others, and even to belong to places. She has subtly mixed habits, traditions inherited from both her families, paternal and maternal, or copied from what she's observed in the families of her friends. Then, she has recreated them in her way, and she has done everything so it could just be that. As a little girl, she went to her Grand-maman and her Grand-papa for Sunday lunches, and every time, she wondered about her other grandparents. Did they also have their other grandchildren over? If there too, one went there on Sunday, dressed to the hilt, to have lunch with people who'd seen us naked because they'd changed our nappies. She would have loved to have had more memories from those moments spent with her Grand-maman and her Grand-papa.

And so as an adult, Stéphanie had instituted these visits to Grandma, which always started with a ritual, which had become a universal ritual of modern days: a selfie. Her Grandma was always game for it, even if she constantly complained of not having the real paper photo. Grandma loved to complain and Stéphanie enjoyed that, because when Grandma wasn't complaining, it meant that she wasn't well.

Anyway, every time Stéphanie visited, her Grandma dressed to the hilt, either alternating with a design sewn out of a wrapper from head to toe, or a maxi skirt and a T-shirt, which, invariably, was always an advertising T-shirt. To tell the truth, Stéphanie had been open-mouthed when she'd seen her Grandma once wearing a Fido Dido T-shirt. White as snow, ironed, and worn to perfection. How had she managed to keep it in such a pristine condition since the 90s?

It just puts you off throwing money at prized and expensive labels like Ralph Lauren, a classic here among Dynamic Young Professionals, so much so that every time she saw a man wearing a polo T-shirt with that horse insignia, oftentimes wearing it with the same boat shoes that her very French classmates from the business schools had worn, she couldn't help smiling to herself whilst thinking, "He's worn his Ivorian uniform."

As for her hair, it was a real topic. Grandma hid hers under a head wrap tied skilfully. And the note of girlie-ness, a touch of colour, often some pink, peeking out of the sandals from each of Grandma's toenails. Grandma was the image of her studio flat in the depth of Yop City: tiny and tidy. Of course, Stéphanie sent those selfies to her father. She'd often said to her psychologist that Oedipus had sent her to Abidjan. That woman appealed to her straight away. She wasn't one of those quiet psychologists who invariably brought the issue back to yourself; rather, she was from the school of "And don't you think that ...?" But, see, she hadn't gone back to the Rue des Jardins – Deux Plateaux Vallon clinic when the psychologist had suggested that perhaps it was that same Oedipus preventing her from finding a man.

Since then, Stéphanie has sworn to herself that she did not miss having a man in her life. She still read *Psychologies*, which she brought back from her work trips, or which she always purchased at FNAC, even if sometimes, it meant getting them a month late. And then, there was her best friend in Paris, with whom she spoke a few times a week. In fact, they spoke about it at length the previous week. Stéphanie had been speaking to Alexandra about that TEDx conference where she'd listened to that young woman introducing herself as a *"célibattante"* rather than a *"célibataire"*; not just a single woman, but a fighting single woman.

"It is a chic concept, dêh!"

"Why am I not convinced?"

"What aren't you convinced by? My enthusiasm or my attempt at the local accent? You know, you gotta take on some of these expressions. Speaking like a Benguiste ruins you in this country, I tell you." Stéphanie had said before bursting into laughter. Their chats, as it always was the case, went off on a tangent.

"Translation, please!" Alexandra had replied back in English, before laughing.

As they say in Abidjan, "Alexandra, there isn't two of her."

Sitting in front of her computer, Stéphanie had wanted to teleport herself to be with her friend in Paris. At least there was Skype. What's more, internet was working well that evening and they were able to video chat.

"I miss you, my dear."

"Well yeah, I miss you too. So, translate that thing you spoke about earlier." Alexandra smiled and sat up as if she were about to receive an emeritus lecture.

"I mean, if you speak your posh French here, people get it into their mind that you are from Bengué, well, Europe, and that consequently, you're rich. Believe me, prices just go up! In the taxis, at the markets!"

"Dang!" Alexandra burst into laughter. "I'm speechless! Looks like it isn't only in France that people are prejudiced. But I would rather people thought of me as being loaded rather than being a poor woman still swinging from the trees. Depends on what floats your boat." She smiled again.

"Well, you're not wrong there."

"So yes, my *célibattante*, even if I'm not convinced by that thing. But anyway, there you go."

The psychologist had been wrong. Her father didn't have anything to do with the fact that Stéphanie had not found the right man (she'd stopped looking for Prince Charming a long time ago). As for Stéphanie, she was sure of having done a good thing by lying to them all. Thanks to her silence, she'd been able to get ahead.

This evening, with her father in this restaurant, she realises just how proud he is of her and of what she's achieved. He's just met an age mate and has been talking to him about Stéphanie's success story. With just a glance at him however, Stéphanie knows that she won't like André, who is the perfect incarnation of an Illusion Vendor (or better yet, of a HIV – a Hallucination and Illusion Vendor), a feeling confirmed when André asks, or rather advises her, a bit like she does with the suggested products at her E-commerce business, to call him uncle. Just as André gives her his business card, which must be a real sucking hole for young women (André Francis Afangue, AFA consulting, CEO), he turns towards her father and brings out another one of his weapons: humour.

"She now just needs to make you a grandfather."

At that moment, Stéphanie brings out her smile of circumstance, the one that is not too bright, which she does by turning her head sideways. The one she keeps for unfunny jokes delivered by UPs, Untouchables People. People like her boss, or her real uncles and aunties, and those others with whom being honest would be sacrilege, or even a diplomatic incident.

It is after André leaves that she feels as if she's been hit by a dagger. Her eyes have met those of her father, which for a moment, had clouded over. But why has he never told her that he wanted to become a grandfather?

She waited for André to be sufficiently far off before calling the waitress over.

"Could you bring me a glass of Glenfildich?"

Stéphanie knew that Whisky brought forth honest talk. Whether that was in her father, or in herself. She'd established that ritual, even though she never touched a drop. They would sit on the veranda, facing each other, and her father would place a bottle of Glenfildich on the rattan table in front of them. In the humidity of those evenings, true and honest chats had been had. Why he left. Why she returned. Life changes, family expectations, the destiny of the country ... She'd also spoken of her dreams. Dreams that she had within her, and which she looked after, the way others looked after their hevea plantations. A house by the sea, a second home — but nobody used that term here, so she didn't either — in San Pedro or Sassandra. A concept store in Bouaké, which was always referred to as "inland", as if being "inland" was a fatality.

She never saw it that way.

That evening was the first time that Stéphanie was drinking the strong liquor in front of her father. She needed to be able to bear the heartache she will submerge him in. She hoped he would be able to control his anger. How does a father behave when he learns that his daughter has been raped? She would soon know.

She hated herself for crushing him with this confession that would not ease her pain, but she was tired of carrying the weight alone. If he wanted every single detail, she would give it to him.

"Papa?"

"I know."

The List

Aito Osemegbe Joseph

The one I once called my daughter haunts me now. While my family sleeps peacefully before a new day is fully born, she saunters in and tortures me with her soft smile. Up until six months ago, Adaeze's smile did not have such power. Up until six months ago, we all preached the same message to Adaeze, but did she *hear word?*

Marry an Ibo man.

Marry a strong, rich Ibo man.

Marry a man whose parents are Ibo.

She refused.

She would say *Chris is this* and *Chris is that*, that our opinion did not matter. But it came to matter when it was time for the native wedding, the giving away, in her father's compound in Ogudu, Lagos. She was in her bedroom waiting to be called upon. The guests sat under canopies in the field outside the house, already feasting while we, her fathers, made the transactions of *her head*, deciding her fate.

The decision-making shouldn't have been harder than it usually was, but for goodness' sake, her Chris did not even know that "*mba*" meant "no", and all he wanted was a "yes" from us. I taught him the word and the first sentence he makes with it?

"*Mba*, sir, we don't live in America," he said, interrupting me. "We're from London and we live right there, sir."

I just smiled and pretended not to notice his mother nudge him in the side. I decided to put the arrogant boy in his place. After all, when a child rubs his father's face with fingers extracted from the anus, then is the right time for a merciless beating of those buttocks.

"Young man, don't you know that when an Elder farts, the children around must perceive the smell in silence? Whether it is London, Canada, Italy, Portugal, China or Japan, everything is 'America'. A white man's land is a white man's land." As I spoke, the whole sitting room erupted in laughter. I wasn't assuaged by the forced laughter. I straightened the paper in my hands (before Chris spoke, we had started verifying the wedding list printed on this paper), turned away from him and faced the dining table, where the gifts were heaped. Adaeze's younger brother, Uchenna, stood beside this heap alongside Chris's younger brother, Oliver. The duo nodded, signifying their readiness to continue the list verification.

"Forty tubers of yam," I called out.

"Complete!" Uchenna shouted, after a meticulous count.

I wondered if the hard times caused by the crash of oil prices had hit London also. No, I prayed it had hit them so bad they would default on at least one of the items. I continued with the list, silently swearing that if just one carton of anything wasn't in that heap, they would smell their behinds.

Two packets of Cabin biscuits.

Complete.

Twenty-four tins of Dusting powder.

Complete.

Five jars of Stella pomade.

Complete.

Ten packets of St. Louis sugar.

Complete.

This far into the list and these people hadn't missed a single item yet. I looked at the young man, Chris or whatever he called himself, his mother, and the hoard of the others who had come from the United Kingdom with him. All of them, speaking as if from their noses, chattering on without respect. I was tempted to tell them to get out of the house and return when they were ready to marry, but the look on the face of Adaeze's father, Mazi Okonkwo, begged me to bear with their interruptions and unwholesome chatter and get it all done with. The old man was tired; he had let his daughter strong-arm him into giving his consent to the marriage. I went on.

Two big-sized Ovaltine.

One carton of Peak milk- powder.

Twenty-four loaves of bread.

Twenty-four cartons of malt.

Two bags of salt.

One big tray of stock-fish.

One 25kg keg of palm oil.

One 25kg keg of groundnut oil.

One 25kg keg of kerosene.

They had brought two kegs of palm oil, groundnut oil and kerosene each.

"This is insulting. We asked you people to bring one keg and you bring two? Are you saying you know more than us? Or you think we are begging you people?" I asked Uchenna and Oliver to shift the extra kegs towards Chris's people. Even though I noticed that Chris's jaw was tightly clenched and he was silent all the while, his people apologised for the oversight, and I forgave them and went on with the list.

A basket of onions.

Two 25kg bags of rice.

One thousand and fifty naira for the bride price.

One thousand five hundred naira for the village youths.

Ten thousand naira to *bring the pot down from fire.*

I didn't care if they understood what "bringing the pot down from fire" meant. I saw no reason to explain. They want to marry an Ibo girl and they can't speak Ibo. Nonsense. When they come for our festivals and parties, will they call me to come sit beside them to interpret? Common sense should tell them that for more than two decades we have cooked a delicious meal; it is not empty hands we'd use to bring the pot down.

Two big-sized stainless steel basins.

Two big umbrellas.

Two George materials.

Two Hollandis materials.

Two blouse materials.

Two head ties.

One wristwatch.

Two pairs of shoes.

One big box.

One lamp.

One handbag for the mother of the bride.

Six yards of Nigerian wax.

Pa Ezekiel, the oldest amongst us, the man who was to give the village's blessing on the couple, looked worn out too. The edge of his lips curved downwards and his eyes were distant as if he was looking at the future of the union of these two very different families. Like the rest of us, he had tried to convince Adaeze to avoid this mistake by bringing good men to her feet, threatening and raising hell, reminding her of the fate of her cousin Uluomachi, who had married a Yoruba man and had become his mortar, only good to be pummeled with the pestles he called his hands. But our Adaeze didn't *hear word.*

The boy, Chris, was as black as any Uchenna or Chibueze could be and he would have passed for one, until he let words roll off his quick tongue. His best man was even worse. This one spoke so fast, I doubted that he could understand himself. *Fiafiafiafiafia*, their tongues went, yet they had never known the joys of *nsala* soup or of the legendary Ogbono soup. These ones hadn't begun living. They had been fortunate to win Adaeze's heart in the one year she had spent studying in the United Kingdom, opting for her instead of their lean girls that look like starved thirteen-year-old boys. It was a good thing for them, surely, but we couldn't say the same thing for Adaeze or for us, her family.

Our Adaeze had come back with a master's degree in Operations Management and a boy. This boy, Chris. I let my eyes linger on the scar that made a short dash across his left cheekbone. Had he earned that in a brawl? Was the scar a gift from a disgruntled lover he had beaten up? But our Adaeze refused to see these things. She was the stubborn fly that was following the corpse right into the grave. Even the good book said, "There is a way that seemeth right unto a man, but the end of it is destruction thereof."

Adaeze would say, "But, Uncle, you're not my father." She failed to accept that I was her father and she was daughter to every single one of her uncles, even to Chibueze, who was younger than her. She knew that among us Ibos, when an arrow kills game, the hide is for the shooter but the meat is for all, and that when we marry a person, we marry the family also. But Adaeze had chosen to bring meat that was hard to chew; horsemeat when there was goat meat and chicken all around. She didn't realise that this stupid decision of hers would break her father's heart and mine as well.

I remembered my conversation with Adaeze's father the night before, as we sat at the backyard and stared into the dancing flames of the firewood over which the women cooked in preparation for the festivities.

"My brother, I have decided to accept my daughter's decision, but I still have concerns. Has Adaeze thought of how Chris will cope during Christmas celebrations in the village? When young men of his age-grade compete in wrestling matches, will he join them or be in a corner smoking his American cigar? Will he join us when we all gather to eat from the same bowl? When we roll perfect balls of hot *garri* with our trained palms, will he ask to use a fork?" The crackle of burning wood filled the night as he shook his head in worry. "How will he and his people handle our ways?"

I had no reply for him, but those words stayed with me. I wasn't sure Adaeze understood these things the way we did; the complexities of multiracial family relationships. But these were the simple problems Mazi Okonkwo had raised. The hard ones made me shudder. What would she do when she had to flog her child to correct some wrongdoing and Chris disagreed? They would begin to argue what child abuse is and what it isn't. How would they cope with our loud and ecstatic version of Christianity? When the young boys jam their hands non-stop in rhythm with the drum beats and then Mama Nkechi starts rolling on the floor, howling and screaming *in the spirit*, would they even understand? How would they feel when they were at one of our parties where no one ever remembers to speak English?

I had done everything I could to dissuade Adaeze from *mixing blood* with these strange people right until that moment when I read out the list. I continued reading, slow and sad, dreading every second that brought the impending doom closer.

Ten thousand naira for the siblings of the bride.

Complete.

One carton of Canoe soap – the unwrapped one.

Complete.

One thousand, two hundred and fourteen naira for the mother of the bride.

Complete.

Two big goats.

"Tied to the mango tree in the backyard," Oliver called out.

We couldn't accept word-of-mouth testimony, so a delegation of six had to go confirm; three from our family and three from theirs. But before we went to the backyard, I gave another speech.

"All these things on this list and our strict adherence to it is not us selling our daughter out to you. It is tradition that has been passed down for centuries."

After a round of applause, we proceeded to the backyard to check the goats, and till today I wish things had gone differently.

When we reached the tree where the goats were tied, I saw an opportunity but the words came out of my wife's mouth first.

"Eeeehhhhhhh, what is this? We asked for goats and you people are here with rabbits." She struck her open mouth with her palm repeatedly, making mocking noises.

"Blimey! Fighting over the size of goats? What kind of primitive people are these?" Oliver blurted, unable to rein his disgust.

"Primitive? You call us primitive? Do you have Elders where you come from? You just disrespected these grey hairs on our heads, but I don't blame any of you. I don't. You have come all the way from London to play but now you can see there are no swings and bouncing castles around..."

"What's this codger saying? Bollocks!" Oliver shot out, rudely interrupting me while breaking free from his mother's withholding grasp. "What's so bloody special about their daughter, yeah? My brother just had to want a minger, yeah?"

Adaeze's brothers and cousins fired back immediately, flinging curses without restraint. "Look at you people. *Blowing big-big grammar on top empty pockets.* Simple bride list you cannot bring and you're *opening rotten mouth* to insult your generation," Uchenna blared.

Chris's people didn't hold back either. They joined Oliver in hurling slurries of nasal retorts interspersed with "innits" and "gonnas" and "yeahs". Insults that we barely understood anyway. In all of these, Chris and his mother remained quiet.

The guests close enough to hear the squabble joined us at the backyard and the sound of angry voices escalated. I noticed Adaeze at the backyard window, peeping. She jumped out of view when our eyes met.

With the loudest voice I could muster, I hushed every other person and spoke the words of doom, "You people should leave here and return when you're ready to marry."

The silence grew intense and I could see Adaeze's father plead with his eyes. Everyone focused on me, and the mouths that were running sharp a moment ago started to quiver. In several past marriages, when we got to this point the begging would begin. They would kneel and make several promises and then I, the Whirlwind of Umuchoke, the speaker of the village, would tell them to calm down. I would tell them that the marriage list is part of our culture, and that the haggling was designed to build rapport between the marrying families. I would give this speech, round up with the marriage list and move on to the prayer of the oldest clan man. This was our way.

But, these people did not beg. I watched the angry looks on their faces transform into shock. I hid my own surprise. Had they not thought to bring someone along to tell them how we did these things? Someone old and wise enough to advise them on the right way to please their future in-laws? Someone with sense? I watched the boy's face tighten, his teeth clenching on his lower lip and his jaws pulsing. At that moment, he didn't look like a little boy any more. The fire in his eyes blazed and fear gripped me, the kind felt when a madman walks towards one, frowning and wielding a large stick. No one attempted to break the silence and it seemed everyone's gaze had shifted to Chris. We watched as the boy stretched trembling hands towards the backyard door, towards Adaeze. Our gaze followed him, and we caught the tears on Adaeze's face before she backed out of view again.

Chris walked boldly into the house and like an animated crowd we followed him. When we got into the sitting room, we saw that Adaeze had her arm in his, as they walked towards the front door.

We followed them outside and stood, watching as they passed the surprised crowd seated under the canopies, past the compound gate and out of sight. It was at this point that we woke up. Mazi Okonkwo, Adaeze's father, was the first to bolt for the gate. I followed quickly and I heard many footsteps and murmurs behind me. It was barely ten seconds after Adaeze and Chris stepped out, but we didn't see them anywhere along the street, and that was the first of the unfortunate events to come our way.

At first, all we felt was rage. We shooed Chris's people outside the compound and for the next few days we tried to get over the insult of Adaeze and her stupid boy walking out on the family and all the guests. I was the family's hero. I had told the cheap Londoners off and upheld our pride and culture. Over the next few days, all the family members returned to their homes. Some returned to our place in Umuchoke village, others returned to places as far away as Kano but most of us who were now based in Lagos didn't have far to go. I was the last to leave Mazi Okonkwo's compound, because we were neighbours and I just needed to walk around the fence.

When Adaeze refused to return home after one week, things changed. Faces frowned whenever I showed up, and whispers hushed when I stepped into a room. The faces of those who had supported me in sending Chris's family off became coloured with disdain.

My wife would mutter and grumble when she returned from the nearby hair salon, relaying gossip. "I heard that Mazi Okonkwo's wife has been saying you are jealous of her daughter's success, and pride pushed you to take a poor decision." She would refuse to look me in the eye while saying these things. "You really should have stopped them from leaving." The other day she came home crying after watching in dismay as Uchenna swore to disrupt the weddings of our daughters in fair revenge. "Go and beg your brother," she pleaded. "You did wrong. Accept it like a man and go and beg all of them, please."

Adaeze sent a Facebook message to Uchenna two weeks after her disappearance: *Tell em gudbye.* When Uchenna relayed the message to the rest of the family, there was wailing. Adaeze's mother held my shirt to the neck, pushed me against the wall and shook me violently, demanding her daughter from me. Mazi Okonkwo asked that I leave their house and only return if I was sent for. My own wife and children gave me foul glances and took sides with the rest of the world. For goodness sake, I had only done what I always did. I had only spoken the mind of every true Ibo man.

After loads of messages the family sent to Adaeze via Facebook and email, she replied with another Facebook message, much longer than the previous one, and even though Mazi Okonkwo didn't let me see it I knew the details from overhearing them talk about it. Adaeze had moved with Chris to Berlin, Germany, and wasn't sorry for walking out on us. She had gotten a job with KPMG, an auditing firm, and was looking to begin a PhD programme soon. And, most shocking, she was two weeks pregnant.

No one complained that an unmarried girl was pregnant; instead, they offered a thanksgiving Mass on her behalf, praising God for her safety. The messages came in fortnightly and the reading became a regular part of our family's monthly meetings. Uchenna's phone would be passed from person to person while *nsala* soup and *garri* went around in trays. They admired her Berlin pictures and read the messages with joy, but somehow the phone never got to my hand. No one was sure how much more havoc I could cause by touching the phone or seeing the pictures. I didn't complain; satisfied with hearing them talk about our estranged daughter.

It was six months after Adaeze's disappearance that I saw her again. In the early hours of the morning, before the darkness drifted away with the cock's crow and before the noise of crying babies and clanking pots filled the air, she walked in through the door, smiling at me. She didn't say a word but her smile told me a thousand things. It told me that she had learnt her lesson and would come back home to marry a proper Ibo man. I smiled in response and like a fading dream she walked out of the door as quietly as she had come in. Same time, every morning, she visits and together we go over that terrible day.

We talk about how things could have turned out differently.

"I'm worried about you," my wife said to me two nights ago as we lay in bed. "You talk in your sleep. You walk around, talking to yourself. Every minute *Adaeze this, Adaeze that. Biko*, I am worried."

I stared at the lowered flame of the kerosene lantern on the table, her words echoing in my mind. *Adaeze this, Adaeze that.* Was I slowly running mad because of guilt? No way, *Tufiakwa*! I did what was right.

When I didn't reply, my wife hissed and turned around to face the wall. "My own is, stop this behaviour! And don't wake me up with your mumbling and grunts again — that is the work of the goats in the backyard."

It's 4am in Ogudu, Lagos. I lie in bed, my wife's back warm against my body, and watch Adaeze walk in through the door again. Her smile is derisive but it will not dissuade me from reminding her of all the warnings we gave her. I will also tell her of the fire she has kindled: how Nneka, her cousin, introduced a Hausa man and no soul complained; how Uchenna dared to say he wants to join a dancing group and no one told him to go read his books. How even my own teenage daughter has started *raising shoulder*, talking to boys across the street in my presence. I will ask Adaeze if this madness is what she wants. I will paint this growing discord properly and show her the fire that's now raging simply because she refused to *hear word*.

The Swahilification of Mutembei

Abu Amirah

Mutembei keenly observes Mombasa beneath the inexorable sun, a town clinging on its designated part on the warm palms of Mama Africa trying, like any other metropolitan is wont, to curve a niche for itself against an absurd level of expectations.

Youthful dreams smashed against the jutting rocks on the shores with a promise that others who dare share connatural dreams will suffer the same pitfalls and abstraction.

An Ocean the smell of slavery, broken promises, Portugal and Vasco Da Gama's piss, washing away hopes and aspirations, so much so that new generations have nothing which resembles their ancestors' footsteps to fit or surpass.

Swahili Nights skewered skillfully, ducking between ghawha cups, rising up with the scented Oud which bears the prosody and cadence of Arabic nights, to meet an enthusiastic, vibrant culture; a culture that thrives on the backs of ancestors who look on with less alacrity.

Yet beneath all these and the uncanny ability of the aforementioned fireball to offer a sacrificial, ephemeral lamb to camera lenses in the form of unforgettable sunsets and adorable sunrises, the city thrives and lives to make a better tomorrow from a wounded past.

The view is as breath taking and contagious as the touch of a fleeing lover, who in her routine disappearances leaves one with the anticipation that indeed tomorrow, if it ever comes, will hold better and perhaps more compelling narratives than yesterday.

"You know something, Mutembei?" Nasoro quips.

"Tell me," Mutembei says, pushing an inverted bottle top across the board. He makes a face as he sips the bitter, ginger flavored *Kahawa Chungu*.

"While everything spikes out with age, your game funny enough seems to deteriorate."

"Is that so, that everything grows with age?" Mutembei asks.

"*Naam, Kila kitu,*" Nasoro remarks. "Everything apart from your wife's love for you. That, my friend, never grows!"

"Is that an admission that you are lonely because your wife no longer loves you?"

"Which one? I have three wives, remember!" Nasoro winks.

"Compounded loneliness," Mutembei says. "No wonder you have been so grumpy lately."

Nasoro grunts, taps on the drafts board with his piece, striding over Mutembei's cowering pieces, three of them, ultimately holding them hostage with several others on his side.

Mutembei winces. *How will I ever beat this old timer?*

"A point comes in life when you can no longer say that your partner loves you or vice versa; it's more than love, perhaps we could call it…" pausing a moment, piece held in the air like an eagle, to study his opponent's apparently weak position on the board, "a sympathetic appreciation of the role that you play in that partnership, and the undeniable knowledge that that person, in spite of his or her peculiar characteristics is the right one for you."

He knew all about Nasoro's three marriages from which he had been wonderfully blessed with fourteen children, three miscarriages and four cats; and he had maintained a perfect balance of sanity throughout. Mutembei figured he would have lost his mind already if he was in his shoes or bed for that matter; but Nasoro kept growing stronger with age!

"*Nyumba ndogo raha*," Nasoro used to tell him. "Ever since I got the third I feel like I am indeed growing younger. She makes me honey and milk every morning my friend, now am stronger than an ox from Rift Valley!"

"Honey and milk?" Mutembei would ask, almost always over a game of drafts under the ageless, timeless shadow of a *Makuti* roof. "What's special about it?"

"Aah," Nasoro would say. "While you younger men have your vigor and vitality, we older men have our secret weapons. Or why do you think young women prefer old men?"

"Wealth, most likely, and the endearing prospects of a good inheritance?"

"No. Start taking honey and milk and you will discover why old men still sire children even at ninety!"

Mutembei had first come to Mombasa in the infant nineties after dropping out of high school courtesy of Mwiti, a friend who had gotten into the *miraa* business while still very young; and had whispered into his ear of profitable exploits in Mombasa, as vast as the ocean itself.

"Take for instance the last trip I made on Tuesday," Mwiti had explained. "I only had two sacks of *miraa* but made enough to add the tally to four sacks for my next trip this coming weekend. *Hii maisha yanataka ujanja*, Vaite. Now I have loyal customers already who are never content until they get my Khat."

Mutembei nodded slowly, the sheer weight of his thoughts in the face of such profits weighing down his chin.

"In case you haven't noticed," Mwiti had continued. "I've built a decent house for my parents already and soon I will be moving out of my *Thingira*!"

"Has your father given you a piece of land to build on already?"

"*Kitambo sana!*" Mwiti said, throwing his hand back to give an impression of how long ago he got his land. "You know once you prove that you are a real man, your father will welcome you into manhood by giving you a share of his property."

Mutembei's father was a primary school teacher and it went without saying that he wanted his son to follow suit. He was sitting on a twelve-acre piece of land which he'd inherited from his deceased father, and Mutembei didn't need a logarithm table to calculate how much land he stood to inherit

"I will be getting married soon too," Mwiti had announced.

"Married?" Asked a shocked Mutembei.

"*Sindio*," Mwiti shrugged. "What else is there for a man making his own money to do other than get married?"

"But you are still very young!"

"That's where you're wrong my friend," he patted him on his shoulder. "Money makes you mature quicker because you have the power in your pocket!"

Mutembei remained restless for the entire week as he pondered over Mwiti's good fortune. True, he had built a very good house for his parents, which so happened to be the envy of all villagers. Women talked about it in their *Chamaa* meetings while men, hurdled in their drinking dens, mingled it with their bitter illicit liquor.

He thought about school and his father's dream that he, too, would become a teacher one day; though it was hardly what he wanted to do with his life. He considered a teaching profession to be too Napoleonic, ridiculously dwarfish and an unjustly rewarding activity which would, without a doubt, impose upon him a case of chronic dissatisfaction at the thought of living a life without purpose- inhaling chalk dust his entire life to cough out teachers and lawyers, pilots and doctors, more teachers and blue and white collared robbers, all of whom ended up with more fulfilling lives than his. Ultimately, he would probably die from chest infection.

Such a sorry life!

He desired to be a writer since he had a way with words. Prose and poetry made his heart race and on many occasions he had placed himself in the shoes of great wordsmiths like Edgar Allan Poe, Mark Twain, Charles Dickens and Jane Austen though he had struggled a bit with *Sense and Sensibility*. Writing was life, capturing every moment and immortalizing it in the capsule of an adjective and it was through it that he could create a world of his own filled with wordy rainbows flawlessly pinned to the sky.

"Writer *kitu gani?*" His father had spat angrily when he mentioned his desired brand of lunacy. "How do you expect to make a living from that?"

"By writing!" He answered too fast. The words were wiped clean from his mouth with a slap.

"That is not a career I want for you," his father cautioned. "Being a teacher is God's way of giving you the power to shape the lives and destinies of the people you teach and the joy and satisfaction comes from seeing the product of your labor become something meaningful in life. Nothing good will ever come from being a writer."

But there is father, he wanted to point out. *Prolific writers like Ngugi wa Thion'go have made it big and ironically, they are now teaching the native English speakers to use their language. And Meja Mwangi, Achebe, Soyinka, Grace Ogot and David Mailu. I want to follow their path, father, I really do. My satisfaction will come when I see the words I create blossom into splendid flowers that everyone smells and enjoys in this path of life...*

But the slap had rendered all his arguments meaningless.

"So, when are you getting married?" Nasoro asked him as he rearranged the pieces on the drafts board again for a third round of decimation, plunder and victory.

"Not anytime soon."

"Why? Doesn't your *mzungu* darling want to get married anymore?"

"We will get married. Everything in its due time."

"Of course," Nasoro said, nodding. "But if you permit me I can talk to my fellow *wazee* and we can get a good Swahili girl for you.

Your *mzungu* shows no signs of ever coming back." He had been thinking for quite some time now about marrying off one of his daughters to Mutembei, mostly because there was no favorable suitor among the young men whose families had approached him.

But then again, there were a whole lot of factors that currently hindered him from raising the suggestion to Mutembei.

Mutembei laughed.

"You are growing older as the days pass and I think it is time you forget about your blonde-haired fiancé." Nasoro explained. "Besides, you have lived among the Swahili people long enough to warrant you the right to marry here."

He knew Nasoro was right and it had become clear to him too that Cindy had probably forgotten him. They had had what seemed to be a very promising future with a possibility of settling in Delaware once they got married; she to continue with her Documentaries and painting, while he pursued writing in the hope of publishing an anthology-poetry or otherwise, someday.

Cindy had left with a bearded American photographer, with a camera lens the size of a Giraffe neck, for the Mara and Serengeti to film Cheetahs and Lions for National Geographic and that was the last he saw of her. Not that she was mauled by a Lion or anything, she just fell head over heels in love with Fauna and memories of him were replaced with an undying, rapacious fascination with nature. The emails no longer bore any semblance of the passionate fire they once shared, but of images of animals doing mundane things like licking their paws, with the same being emailed to a thousand other people too!

"But having lived here still doesn't give me that exclusivity to marry a Swahili woman," he said. "The Swahili are a very cultural people who prefer marrying from within the set up. Far as marriage is concerned, I will still remain an outsider."

"But you break bread with them, why would you consider yourself an outsider?"

"Breaking bread is a universal human need—"

"So is the need to build bridges to cross the racial divide."

"Am not sure I follow—"

"Become a Swahili, break down those stereotypical racial barriers, and prove that we are all one regardless of our skin color or place of origin." Nasoro said.

"Ostensibly yes, but I cannot rearrange my origins and genetic impressions to make them Swahili—"

"Leave that to me," He sighed as he signalled the start of the decimation on the drafts board.

Mutembei imagined many things. Living among the Swahili was one thing, but to become one was a different thing. He still swore unmatched allegiance to his upcountry home in Meru while also fighting a raging emotional battle, trying to reconcile with his father's spirit, which seemed to etch itself on every thought he had of home. He just couldn't bid farewell to his spirit without appeasing it appropriately.

"Anyone who drops out of school to pursue foolish dreams is not worthy of being my son," his father had warned him when he broke the news that he would be leaving school to start a *miraa* business in Mombasa. "Never set foot in my property ever again. In fact, don't even come to bury me when I die!"

And his father had remained adamant throughout the years in spite of his mother's constant pleas to tone down. He proved his seriousness when he turned Mutembei down after he had been arrested in Mombasa for allegations of being a member of an outlawed sect which sought secession from what they called *Bara*, Mainland Kenya. Were it not for his mother, Mutembei would have spent the better part of his youth in jail, and just like that the feud between father and son, which sadly lasted until the former's death, began in earnest.

As a way to reconcile with his father's spirit, he started writing a book about a brilliant boy who, as a result of peer pressure, denounces his citizenship on Planet Earth for the promise of a better life on Mars with a blue-eyed woman who jumps ship and leaves him to traverse the Galaxy with only a rodent for company. Then it becomes a rat race, each trying to eat the other for survival, but the boy cannot bring himself to nibble on the rodent's tail, yet the situation prevails upon him to do so. The protagonist in his book is called Joshua and he hopes that through Joshua's journey he will finally put his father's ghost to rest.

"Take me through the basics of becoming a Swahili," he told Nasoro who was busy as always studying his next decimation moves on the board.

"Oh, it's quite simple," he explained. "First lesson you need to learn is how to tie a Sarong. Second..."

"A *kikoi*?"

"Yes. Why?"

"The last time I tried wearing that thing it started slipping from my waist while I was talking to a lady—" He laughed. "That would have been utterly embarrassing!"

"Your problem is that there is just so much of a villager in you that I have given up hope of ever eradicating it. How can you wear a *kikoi* with no underwear?"

"For the record, I had underpants. Let's skip the first lesson, not applicable to me unless I wear them with suspenders. Second?"

"Second you become a Muslim."

Silence.

A generator hums incessantly in the distance.

The wind strides by, carrying in its wake the fury of honking *matatus* calling for passengers in the Business District.

"Do I have to?"

One of the reasons he was allegedly charged with being a member of an outlawed sect was his friend Mwiti, who had joined several of such groups, ending up, as rumor had it, in Somalia as an Al Qaida affiliate fighter. The Police had been on Mutembei's back for quite a while, closely associating him to being a member too- an accusation he escaped through sheer luck.

And his fear was that being a Muslim, much as terrorism wasn't a Muslim monopoly, would draw the Security Agents' interest in him again. He had heard stories from Mombasa residents-victims of arbitrary detention and renditions on terrorism-related charges, of the torture that they had gone through.

Water boarding.

Electric shocks.

Crushed dreams and genitalia.

He knew he wouldn't last a day if ever he was arrested. He would rat out anyone and everyone he ever knew, starting with all his phone contacts and friends he remembered from Kindergarten!

"Well," Nasoro explained. "Not really. There is no compulsion in religion. Your religious allegiance is a matter that only you can decide for yourself."

Nasoro was disappointed. Unbeknownst to Mutembei, Nasoro had a son whom he rarely talked about. He had heard people call him Abu Musa- father of Musa, but he never at any time asked him who Musa was since none of his children had that name. He presumed it was one of his many nicknames. Musa had been recruited as a Somali-based fighter, leaving behind a disappointed father who had been safe in the knowledge that he would leave behind a worthy heir, and a grieving mother who cried for his son every night.

At first, Nasoro had blamed the Government for Musa's recruitment into a terrorist group. It was the Government that had marginalized the Coastal people by failing to provide proper schools and resources to improve the state of learning. Musa had tried on several occasions to get employed, but the more learned, better equipped, more favored upcountry people got the best jobs and the locals like Musa were left to eat the crumbs. Nasoro had eventually quit the finger pointing once he realized that while only one finger pointed at the Government's fault, three other fingers were inadvertently pointing back at him.

Nasoro loved Mutembei as if he was his own son right from the moment he walked into his famous Biryani Café several years back looking for a job, any job. This was after everything he owned had gone down the drain when he got arrested.

"Fair enough," Mutembei said.

"But you can still pick a Muslim name to be identified by." Nasoro masked his disappointment with a smile, a luxury only enjoyed by the wise. "A name like Hemedi."

"Hemedi?" Mutembei repeated the name several times, whispering it, savoring it in his tongue, perceiving of it in upper and lower case letters, as a signature on a bank cheque, trying to match his core values to it. "Sounds alright," he said. "But isn't the name common only among the people from Lamu?"

"So what?" Nasoro pushed a cap on the board. "Will they sue you for using it?"

"I guess not," Mutembei answered, holding his inverted bottle top to jump over Nasoro's pieces, holding the vanquished ones hostage on his lap. "But don't you think it's rather odd a dark skinned guy from upcountry Meru answering to that name?"

"I didn't know names had a tribal or pigment affiliation too. I thought that was only a reserve for our political selves!" Nasoro replied studying the drafts board. "Okay, choose one of your own liking then," reeling from the shock of having so many pieces taken at once.

"Third lesson?" It was his time to study and anticipate Nasoro's move.

"Identify wholeheartedly with the Swahili culture, history and problems."

He could easily identify with the culture but history and problems were a different brew of *kahawa*. The culture had already adopted him and he had no qualms with that. His own history with his father and the problems he went through trying to reconcile with him prior to his death kept him from adopting other people's problems.

He would only become Swahili after he had adequately appeased his father's spirit, giving it an appropriate send off. Joshua was the vessel he was using to bridge the gap between him and his senior's spirit and he would wait until Joshua had fought his battles in Space- which hinged on a very thin line between precaution and paranoia, so he could fight his when he got back to earth.

Until then, he would only be partly Swahili as he nursed the notion of at least taking valuable lessons on how to tie a Sarong.

POETRY SHORTLIST

Five Poems

Gbenga Adesina

Soft Song
(For Yetunde*)

There is a city in me, the pillar
of which is the love of a child.
A private acre of
history. Tender. So tender. I love
you. I love you so.
how my body is the memory of your
eyes. Child, night rivers through your eyes.
I fall into this river, fall into this rain. I take

your loam, the soft of it, I cross the sea into
where you are night's pulse.

You said, son be strong, fight like a
woman. Water resolves all things.
So, I slink into a city in my skin
where I'm both bird and song; kiln and alluvial.
I bring out a reed, this sliver, song
soft, moist.

*In the sacred knowing of the Yorubas, it is believed that kind mothers, after their own lifetime, often return to the family as a child. So that in the sound the new child makes one also hears the keen of the departed mother.

Hiding Place

I walk into a bar in South Sioux
And it's a city of closed doors.

Bear faced men and women in corduroy pants;
ashen walls and dim lights like loss.
A cloven tongued singer writhes on the floor inside a stereo, the
soft of his sad
calls the soft of my sad by name. The bar walks into me.
I have come here in search of a bird's cry for Ramah.
I walk through the crusted floor with the distinct feeling
of being followed by air. I perch on a stool with a leg that loops
like a family tree.
On the dance floor, an old man and woman hold on to each other
like
God's last promise on earth. They waltz slow.
Their eyes are kind. Each one the song the other dances to. They
do not say a word.
And I, in that instant, saw my father flicker past in their silence.
He's gaunt like love in his starched soldier uniform. He says to
My mum, "Do not cry, I'll be back," and walks into
the silence that would not give him back.
A lady walks up to me, whispers that her
hands would be kind tonight. She says why are your
eyes not children of this country. I open my mouth to
talk, and He, my father, walks out of my tongue.
Who knew he had been hiding in
my mouth. The sable
Birches of vowels, the saffron dusk of tongue.

Hands that do not forget

(For Kofi Awoonor)

In Gudu, south of Apotema, east of all things,
a story stands like a statue,

an urban rendering I'm told is true:
a band of insurgents, woke in the unlight of

one morning and thought it now a sin, an
iniquity of the eyes, that people should carry songs

with such wetness in their iris.
And though they couldn't exactly name what

sort of sin it was – against the flesh or the spirit – they promised
to check their books, but in the interim solved the city by fire;

fed ivy into wells, lashed men in public squares,
railed against dancing or looking or seeing:

an initiation into what they said was a holy blindness.
They raised barricades against the transgression of laughter,

plucked out tongues so that lovers could not call out to lovers,
put ears to doors at nights to sniff out the sin of rhythm

or music: here was the kingdom of silence.
But habits of the eyes do not die young, or do they?

For in the cool of the day's departure,

a woman could be seen, perched on a mound,

gazing with eyes that were not eyes into
the night's cathedral of lights

or her lover beside her, strumming his banjo,
the sin of rhythm, a trance, a fluting that rises

and dips as though in a slow dream
and the insurgents startled by the music, alarmed

at the stirring in themselves, the sin of rhythm, wondered
what was in the music that pierced like salt.

Holy bodies

The hum of the body; subtle accents of hips
when twirled in Kalabari dance. The mellow seduction

of Umteyo, soft rise of chest, slow twist,
call of flesh to flesh.

The secrets the waist keeps to itself
but only reveal when you twirl it into

a song. The body as a slow song.

I see her even now: Mother,
her pockmarked face like innocence, like water,

a little Benin girl again.
In this dream or vision she stoops. Her father:

Abulema, bare-chested sculptor with hands quick
to love as to wood is nursing a bronze slab into

a god. There is a waiting in his eyes. He starts
to make a fluting sound. Music flutes into the air

like a bird.
Mother folds herself into a song and starts

to twirl. Mother.
She would carry her father's songs in her eyes. She

would love the smell of wood as
he carved. She would

choose to dance. She would have those eyes,
always with kindness for me. She would

not dance for Fela. She would not change the world.
She would hear voices, screaming, sweating in her sleep. I would
be six, Kaito twelve.

They would take her away, misdiagnose her. Inject
her with that thing that froze her body. The Pentecostal

neighbours would say it was just a given, seeing
how she danced the dance of demons. Father

would take Kaito and I to the intensive
care unit where tubes snaked into Mother's

nose and her body had become a
cage that trapped her inside. I would

fracture into four, screaming, crying, pulling
at her, trying to wake her up. Father and some

of the nurses would try to hold me; some of them
would start to cry. I would ask,

in tears, how on earth a body so holy
could be broken. Mother.

Her dance, like her mother's
and mothers' before her,

would not be a dance of the body.
It would be more. Mother.

Open
(For K)

The things she says to me
I hide in stones.
Opal, sapphire, etchings like
pressed magnolia.
Eyes are the inner light of prophecy.
Let me be Orpheus. Sculpt O out of Oma
My woman is in the other room
translating Swahili into silence.
The alphabets curl like loss.
The vowels yodel, they open like the love of a child.
The things I say to her she keeps in olive
or wind, rain or the cities of my skin as they
open like the
Love of a child.

Five Poems

Okwudili Nebeolisa

muse

your harelip
not sunset
maggots hiding in garbage
not the butterflies they become
not the moon
my mother sleeping on the couch
not my sister's anger
songs
not hip-hop not rock
shafts of light through the glass
not dreams
my mother again with her stories
not films not me
the baby's hand in the rubble
not the marchers
the rubble covering her breasts
not the noise
the baby finding the nipple
not the dark
the trees disappearing in it
no not you
but your harelip

book-ish ode

books as ageing archivists, holding
your hands, guiding you through a dark stairway.

books with a lot of missiles in them,
books i refused to touch, books with pages

floating in a sink filled with water,
books waiting for you to fall in love with them,

the books my brother lured me to read,
books standing on a shelf, some on tripods,

announcing their ignored presence in the room.
books that light the room, books that cast a shade

like a tree in the day and screamed at night,
made from recycled paper and human spirit.

finding his body

after the explosion, all we saw of him
was his helmet and the monocular
strapped to it; an hour passed before
one of us found an eyeball, then another
his feet both twenty metres from the scene.
i feared what i might find would be his gut
like a snake that refused to die in its hole.
but what i saw was his elegant hand
under inch-deep rubble, hands that
had touched me once and i thought my wife
had travelled from nigeria to come and see me.

all her siblings

hafiz, who is always 'on the run', bloodied:
he'll find a home that's warm and welcoming,
shouting, 'a *bautăwasunanrahama*'.
nafisa with her father behind bars:

she will find home like my paintings did.
she will look at egypt from where she stands
with the local telescope, pardon her
if she can't give the names of all her siblings,

if she can't hope to live in a house some day
but she will not stand and take her parents' shame.

it's never a ghost

it's just the trees swaying to the breeze:
by standards this night i'm a bystander.

it's just someone walking home, counting his steps
so he doesn't fall asleep, starting again

at every hundred he makes, at every
streetlight he passes. it's just the glow

of a cat's eyes, it's merely surprised
at the length of your shadow. it's just two dogs

looking for a suitable place to mate.
it's never a ghost, it's nothing spiritual;

everything is particular at this time,
everything begs for grace, everything is free.

SHORT FICTION LONG LIST

A Native Metamorphosis

Farai Mudzingwa

In a partially extended house in Unit 4, Mpumalanga Township, a man wakes up early on a Monday morning and begins a rapid transformation from Sipho Ngubane to Lucky. A gentle transition on the way to work, he eases into it. A boy sits next to him on the bus, dressed all smart and looking sharp, rocking with the motion of the bus.

*

Winter looks up and finds a man's wife waking up in cold darkness. A stubborn mist smothers the valley of a thousand hills. Its elbows heavy on worn asbestos roofs. It seems sent. An embracing sentry posted against hope and ambition. A thick veil impervious to the rarefied air of affluence, daring the gloomy skies to let the sun shine in.

A man's wife stirs, pulls her stocking head-wrap into place and nudges her husband back to his space. She heaves herself up and steps off the bed achingly — slowly, to avoid the dreadful creaking of her bed and her bones. She feels her way to the kitchen and tugs on the cord dangling in the centre of the room. A bare bulb pings to life and stings her eyes. She shields her eyes with one hand and then slowly opens them, scanning around for orientation.

A man's wife potters about the kitchen, pulls out a big black pot, and sets bath water to boil on an old stove. Sleepy Natal roaches stagger out of the drawers and the pot and the stove. The daring stand their ground and get crunched under foot and swatted under hand. The slow tread bath water for a while, throw up a quick prayer, and spasm off to a better roach place. An old stove creaks to life and a big black pot groans warm then hot. She stands for a while and adjusts the thin wrap around her waist.

A few roaches have crawled out of the pot handle and are now frantically running up and down its length. Death is a nuisance. One drops off the rounded edge, lands on the red-hot stove plate and fizzles and pops. Swelling at first then contorting spectacularly. A little puff of smoke then a charred little crisp is all that remains. Another follows suit, then another, and another. One leaps right off and onto the floor — it makes a quick acquaintance with the bottom of her right foot.

There is no more scurrying, leaping or fizzling and popping — just the hissing of the water coming to a boil. Her waist wrap doubles as oven mittens and she hoists the water and carries it to the bathroom.

A metal laundry dish sits expectantly on a harsh concrete bathroom floor. The steaming water gushes into the dish and settles. A broken showerhead looms above — supervising the whole operation. A thin shaft of sunlight points in bravely through a corner of the window, an early scout out to survey the terrain. The mist is rising. The elbows are coming up a bit slower this morning. An omen, perhaps; a foreboding, maybe. She wakes her husband.

Our man alights from the bus and pushes through the squeaking turnstile. And to cure any uncertainty, his boss greets him,

Good morning, Lucky!

Slap on the shoulder. A little show of superiority. A smile flashes across our man's face. *That* smile that comes on of its own accord. It just is.

I see that smile on broken men begging for change on the corner. On men spoken to in a language they do not understand. I see men smile so and it swells a hot rage within me. There is a little bow too, ever so subtle, yet sometimes horribly exaggerated. It complements the smile; and my insides churn a bit. Men spoken about by another group of men smile this smile and cower like little shits. Men above them speak at and about them; never to them.

A man smiles and sighs. His sigh escapes when the smile starts to trouble his mouth. One can only hold that smile for so long before one must relax and exhale. A boy dressed smart and looking sharp observes this grinning buffoonery from a distance.

Sipho sighs and cowers and bows a little.

Good morning, sir... ah, sir... heh heh, sir.

Bab'uNgubane is transformed. Lucky steps to the fore.

*

If one was inclined to leave Unit 4 on a journey, a journey to Unit 2 perhaps, after avoiding the distractions in Unit 3, one is certain to find oneself going down a long road. Dipping and rising, winding all the time, *kaFiveRand* — an informal name, of course. Turns out in the troublesome 80s, a toll of sorts was levied for passage. Self-appointed toll officers would patrol the road, and a weary traveller, going about his business, was required to state his political affiliation. If it was contrary to that of the toll officers, then five rands were politely extracted from the goodness of the traveller's bounty. A traveller's political affiliation was always contrary, by the way.

It is in this delightful part of the township that a hopeful boy wakes up feeling brand new with a toothy grin and morning wood. First day at work and his little brother has wet their bed. A little piss will not dampen our boy's spirit though. No sir! A boy is on fire. He wipes the crusty sleep out of his eyes and braves a shocking, cold shower. Nerves on alert and drying himself frantically, he looks over his mother's efforts. Clean white shirt, folded tie, pressed pants and polished shoes; shirt collar frayed, tie borrowed, pants and shoes mended. With shirt neatly tucked in and laces tied, he stands before the wardrobe mirror and takes a moment to admire his dashing figure. A boy cleans up well.

There is a box of cornflakes somewhere — and just enough for one. A boy knocks out the cereal into a bowl, careful to keep the powdered flakes at the bottom of the plastic bag. He runs some water in the bowl, sprinkles some sugar over it, calls it breakfast then proceeds to shovel it down. A boy steps out and into the street.

*

The internship interview had been a nervous blur. A boy was short of breath, dizzy and slightly off-kilter. He felt he was keeling over to the left. And they kept offering him *tea or coffee*. The lady from Human Resources was cute. She hardly spoke. Just sat there, pen in hand, with an open note pad, but did not write anything. Just sat there ready to write, and not writing. The whole time — just sat there looking cute as hell. Not a word from her pen or her mouth. She had an expression on her; she was straining for significance; defending her presence in the room. And she kept twirling a loose braid. Just kept twirling it — and not writing. The questions were very mechanical: schools attended, college attended, subjects passed, the usual bullshit; and then the one manager — well, he looked cocky enough — just got to the damn point:

How good is your English? Cos English is the main language here.

After the brief awkwardness, a more sensible manager — he was not cocky, but had that manager confidence about him — steadied the ship somewhat:

I think he speaks better English than I do!

This *was* true. Our boy *speaks well* and is proud of it too — been told so whenever he surprises his audience by speaking so well. Madame Human Resources is not amused. She twirls that braid a bit tighter and seems almost about to write something.

There is only space enough for one person who speaks well in this place, and this new recruit had better get this straight, she thinks to herself. Her pen hovers threateningly over her note pad. With the interview panel assured that a boy *speaks well*, the interview is concluded and everyone has tea and goes to work or something.

*

A boy walks down the road, sticks out a finger and a taxi stops. Uncanny how much power a finger wields. One finger, two, a twirl of the finger, a thumb, and an unruly taxi responds in fashion. He steps in. Squeezing. Damn four per squeaking seat. A boy is careful to keep pesky creases off his apparel. At the rank he jumps off the taxi and onto a bus. Almost full, so he takes a seat next to a man with a vacant stare — or maybe he is meditating or dead or something. The man hardly notices him, shuffles absent-mindedly to give a boy space and carries on staring or meditating or whatever. A boy steps off the bus and is amused to see a man walking past him and through the turnstile.

Meditation over, a boy guesses.

*

People walk in clutching lunch boxes and bottles with drinks. Walking in, chatting away and greeting other good law-abiding folk. A reluctant turn through the turnstile; just slow enough to signal entry into work, and just urgent enough to stave off consequence of tardiness. Other people drive in, in nice cars. Stern looks on their faces. No chatting there. No turnstiles either. Just formal greetings, nods and glass doors into air-conditioned buildings. From a safe distance, a boy observes the man from the bus behaving rather oddly while talking to one of the stern people.

*

A man feels Sipho trembling out of sight and realises this is Lucky's territory. He sinks into his chair and feels the edges of his desk. The chair creaks and tilts and threatens to throw him off. Slight reminder perhaps, of his precarious position in the whole scheme of things. Grime on the desk reminds our man that this desk is shared. A roach sniffs around and scurries off furtively.

Few things signify authority like the elevated factory office. One must look up at it – and the other looks down from it. Lucky looks out of the window and down onto the factory floor. He sees the workers in overalls, tinkering away and darting about like little blue ants. Dust masks and heavy tasks. Machines hum and whirr and stop and start. And workers work and work and work, and break, and work again. He swells with a certain pride. Fifteen years from little blue ant to big blue ant supervising little blue ants. His mouth almost breaks into a smile. The corners of his mouth quiver. He yields a little and his lips curve. He feels all warm and fuzzy inside. Except for that cold wet patch where Sipho is squirming around.

At 08:03 the telephone rings abruptly, pulling our man out from his sweet reverie. Telephones are rude instruments. It is a long ring — with a brief pause — then another long ring. An internal call. An external call would most certainly be Sipho's. Our man Lucky does not have business outside the factory. His concern is with the little blue ants. But this is internal, so Lucky steps to the fore. A little mental check and we're in:

Pre-stage supervisor's office. Lucky speaking. May I help you?

Well, fuck me!

This would have pleased the crown right off Queen Elizabeth II's royal head, Cullinan stone and all! Sipho feels gutted. Fair enough — it's still obvious this is a darkie on the line, but, by all that's mighty, and possibly by all that isn't too, Lucky puts on a jolly good Brit accent!

Crikey!

And so the conversation carries on. Our man puts up a good show by all accounts. Lucky is a showman. And like all showmen, he flourishes. By the by, a caller makes his reasons known:

Lucky, we need a box of samples at the reception to be taken to the warehouse... The box is too big for the sales ladies... Please send one of the factory ladies to pick it up.

Now a man gets to thinking. And in a moment he observes a battle within the war. Lucky scans the floor for someone to send while Sipho looks at him in disgust. Sipho sings to himself – just within earshot of course:

A box is too heavy for a lady to carry,

la-da-da dee de-dee-la-da-daa,

and so must be carried by another lady,

la-da-da dee de-dee-la-da-daa!

Lucky slows down a beat. Sipho has a way of striking a nerve. An uncanny ability to bring Lucky crashing down at choice highlights in his day. Lucky ponders over matters for a while. The tune is now ringing in his ears. Sipho's taunt striking a chord. Lucky tells himself this is just work. Sipho hums the tune. Lucky steels himself, convinces himself that this is just how things are. Sipho breaks into chorus again. Sipho understands that many people face the same conflict daily. Sipho whistles his tune in perfect key. Lucky knows deep down he is still the same person. Sipho taps his feet and clicks his fingers. Lucky summons Victoria and sends her to fetch the box.

A man's boss is half his age. Calls out to him, *Lucky*! and a man jumps to; up off the chair, reeling and crashing against the wall. Stands up stiff and attentive, grinning as a man will. Always the grin, always the jump, always Lucky. Sipho grumbles incoherently.

A man's boss slaps him across the shoulders. They are old friends, are Lucky and his boss. And yet Sipho takes note that Lucky has never given a man's boss that same friendly slap across the shoulders. Odd; them being friends and such. And when Victoria steps into the office, with a box *for Lucky*, a man quickly and with much admonishment, reminds Victoria to refer to him as Bab'uNgubane!

Lucky looks back and sees Sipho cowering. To be exact, he *feels* Sipho cowering, for Sipho is hidden well away — a timid, quivering wretch. Lucky smiles and cracks a dry joke with the boss, who either does not hear or does not care, or both. Lucky isn't bothered much. He is with the boss. Sipho mumbles disapproval and tugs at Lucky. Lucky slaps him well away. The irritating little shit makes his presence felt most inconveniently.

*

The day of induction ends with a hearty valediction:

We shall start you off in a production department. Learn fast and how far you go is up to you!

Armed with this impressive empty rhetoric, a blue work suit and descended balls, a boy sucks in a deep breath, holds it a while, lets it linger in there a bit, allows it to stretch out his ribs, a little creak here, a little groan there, strains his chest forward a bit, then releases slowly — audibly through his mouth. A boy pushes the swing-doors open and steps into a colony of little blue ants. A busy colony, this. Lots of scurrying back and forth. Familiar faces, unfamiliar faces, plain faces, angry faces, lazy faces, tired faces, unfriendly faces, friendly faces. All busy, all working. Fussing about loud machines. Darting between moving parts. Ants moving in pairs. One pushing — one pulling. Ants pointing and beckoning.

A light flashes. A siren wails and the machines all shudder and fall silent. Ants flow between machines and stacks. A trickling not much unlike sand through fingers. Tiny rivulets snaking through. And then we see a bottleneck. A little blue estuary squeezing through the swing-doors. End of shift. The lights go off in an instant. A couple of emergency lights blink on, then the swing doors shut after the last blue ant.

All is quiet. Just the distant humming and hissing of the boiler. No ants, no movement, no sounds. Just the man standing up there. Looking down at the factory floor through the large office window. His hands confidently in his pockets, he turns round deliberately, packs his bag, and walks out of sight.

A boy stands still for a moment. A conflict of emotions. The light in the office above goes out and a peculiar sensation comes over a boy. He turns round and follows the little blue ants.

The shift siren sounds and there is much back and forth in the little blue ants' changing rooms. Weaves are adjusted and mirrors straightened. Victoria, Hazel and Pretty are bundled into lockers and MaNdlovu, Sibongile and MaNtini emerge clutching their handbags.

Scent of Palmolive and Lux wafts through. Windows steamed up and cheap perfume gagging innocent throats. All cleaned up, one could mistake the little blue ants for regular folk.

Much chatter around the clocking machine. Little blue ants are not as silent as one would think. Men now stand where little blue ants scurried by. A man observes a peculiar pushing and shoving — a certain urgency. The clocking machine is not going anywhere soon. It has no dinner arrangements and no school run. The little blue ants are not sure why they push and shove. Their homes are not going anywhere soon either. Something about waiting in turn starts a panic. A struggle for position is in full swing. Instinctive perhaps. A necessary skill in circumstances of scarcity; where one's gain is another's loss. And where one loss costs dearly. A most brutish trait in a situation of abundance.

The clocking machine is not going anywhere anytime soon. No plans this evening. And yet instinct perseveres. More elbowing and bracing for precious purchase. A shoe is lost, an elbow thrust and make-up smudged. Victoria breaks a slight sweat. The clock winds down and finally reads 16:30:00. One last act is left. A swift swipe of their clock cards and Mandla, Siya and Bongani present themselves where DM74, DM70 and EM52 stood but a moment before. Beeping and chattering. A mad dash to the exit turnstile.

Our man makes his way through the turnstile and bids a conflicted farewell to Lucky. Sipho stretches out and comes to the fore. He stands tall and eases into the taxi. It has been a long day. One could say it looks like rain and be forgiven for one's pessimism. Thick dark clouds gather ominously over a man's head. He calls it a day.

April's Foul

Le K-Yann

Translated from French, *Poison d'avril,*

by Edwige-Renée Dro

5:30 AM. Dreams vanish and leave the field to reality. The dew of the sky on the grass starts to faint. The night that had set up its camp in the sky beats a hasty retreat before the day that's earning more and more ground in the sky. Dawn reaches up and swallows the last morsels of darkness. The last barks of dogs, the first songs of the cocks, the first chirps of the birds start to get heard. It is at this time that gangsters return home from stealing, looting and killing, and lie down, tired out by a cold and dark night rich in adventures. It is hard to see where this plot of land surrounded by flowers ends.

In this studio, everyone is snoring, drunk on sleep. An almost dead candle ends its life on a padlock lying by the bed. Sékélé is awake. Did he really sleep? A gnawing cold has taken over his body and his bones; his wife having pulled the little blanket over her. The supplications and the intercessions from the churchgoers of a recently established makeshift church across from his very, very modest home, well, shed, break his eardrums. They've been taught that there isn't any interference between Earth and Heaven at this hour. A lot of people have got up before him, to go in search of happiness. He'd slept, tried to sleep, but instead, had deciphered a thousand time, the undulations of the aluminium sheets of his roof before going to bed. Racking his brain to try and find a solution to his problems. Yesterday, they'd gone to sleep with nothing but 200 Francs worth of bread and tea the colour of urine. Milk demands quite a bit of money. The hunting, the fishing and the harvesting of that day had not been fruitful.

Actually, that's often the case here in Kin. He doesn't want the same scenario to repeat itself. He's learned to save. He and his family can survive on 5,000 Francs a week. In the dreams he had had during his sleep, there had only been the spectre of goods, packages, bundles of stuff and other items. He would like it if that could be teleported to reality, but dreams and reality rarely meet. Perhaps today is his lucky day. He's always hoped, never given up the fight, hence the nickname given to him by his friends and acquaintances, Equipe-epola-te. May the team not lose. His job? Unemployed. Actually, no. Hustler. A father to three unfortunate little boys, as he likes to say. He's been living with a woman for so many years now that he no longer bothers to remember. Sat on what he uses for a bed, a mat, he spends a bad half an hour thinking about his fate, about this day, about his condition, and of course, about the probable changes he wishes for his country. Even if his TV has stopped working for years now — cannot afford to replace it — and if his radio lacks batteries — one cannot rely on the National Company of the Enemies of the Light, he gets the news about the political issues of his country at the Street Parliament. Much has been said and written about Dialogue, National Consultations, Policy, and Article 70. The concept has been stretched so much that it has been transformed into "Dialong".

We didn't eat yesterday. We drank. The bread, the coal and the tea that was taken on credit must be paid. It is the first today and he will come to collect his rent for this forsaken hole. They didn't go to school this year. Pati went to school last year. It would have been Samy's turn this year but he didn't get that opportunity. What kind of country is this, where even primary school isn't free? Where even bread needs to be borrowed! Where we don't even know what to do with ourselves. The spectre of misery wanders freely. It is a lie to say that everything is well in the country. There is an unease, huge problems hover. Ah, let me get up lest I dig my own tomb thinking about all this. A man doesn't cry, he fights, searches and finds solutions.

He had reasons to get up; it was the number one rule at the school of hustling. If you want to earn a good living, you must loathe your home. Living is for the brave. Must wake up early in the day, early in the week, early in the month, early in the year. As with the beginning of every year, Sékélé's most ardent wish is that things go well at the beginning of this month. He holds the dream to feed his family, at least today, going as far as wishing that either by divine providence or through coincidence, the surprise of a good trip, which will give him a good sum of money, courts him. He takes a shower and puts on his work clothes, but just as he is about to put his nose outside, he is called back in. The morning hassles have already started. To think that he'd forgotten about them.

"Are you leaving like that, Pa?"

He is unable to believe his ears. "And how do I usually leave?"

"But you haven't said anything!" Samy replies.

"Money doesn't grow under the bed at night, son. You need to go out to look for it. You understand? When it is there, it is there, but the opposite is also true. We didn't eat yesterday because we didn't have money. Wait for me for today. I'm going to put the hooks and the bait in the water. We'll see what it brings. At the school of life, you must bear things. Let's pray to the One Who is above. May He bless me."

"It was the same song yesterday. I've never been given money in the morning by my father to buy spaghetti, fritters or biscuit like other children my age. Our father is different."

Powerless, he doesn't know what to say. He loves his little family. He bends over backwards for them. He wants to look after them, but he is unable to. Poor him. He could even die for them.

Sékélé leaves. His day has already started to go downhill. His boy is not in the wrong. Neither is he. It's life, the country, the State. He asks himself why his parents gave birth to him in Kin and not elsewhere. Why not in Angola or in South Africa, or even in Congo-Brazzaville, or better yet, in the United States since that's a successful place? Why must there be that huge gap between rich and poor? A gap in which there is no middle class. It seems to him that he belongs to a lost generation, left to fend for itself, to create jobs for itself in order to look after their children. What kind of tribal happiness was that! Where those who went to school and those who didn't often find themselves on the same playing field. A town of surprises, a country of realities, where one can have a B.A but sell phone credits, have a degree like Sékélé but end up a rickshaw man. The unemployment rate is always stable. To work has become the least conjugated verb here. A sadder situation than the end of Titanic. Things that aren't dreamt off come to pass and the opposite is not possible. What a paradox! Everyone blames the State, the real (ir)responsible. It is not doing what it needs to be doing. It has already resigned by telling the children to look after themselves. In the social site, no brick has been laid, not even the foundation stone.

Everyone, except the ones in the "system", is calling for help: doctors, teachers, lawyers, civil servants, even street children. The prices of basic foodstuff have been going up for the last 10 years. Money is hard to come by. Orphans die for lack of bread while elsewhere in the same country, buildings come out of the ground. In that arena of suffering, those who can no longer bear it are in the front row; they choose the easy way, shortcuts because the way to happiness is long. They choose the way of an easy buck, hanging, suicide or poison to end their pitiful life, with the feeling of having missed the meeting with happiness. People like Sékélé however fight against difficult realities, they hold onto life with all their might. They are the Nobel prizes of poverty, the gold medallists of suffering, the best Oscars in the category of the real movie of life. www.misery.com is the most visited site. The poverty of the people needs to be studied in laboratory.

The sky has mood swings. Its face is not bright, appetising. There are dark clouds here and there. There could be a downpour. Taking out his rickshaw, Sékélé worries about the weather. Rain costs them a lot in this neighbourhood: lives, kitchen utensils, clothes, furniture, for those among them who have them, and many other things.

Previously called Tiamutubakata, that is, one who braves dangers, it is now called the marsh neighbourhood because of the damages caused by the rain. They are no stranger to the muddy waters or the waste waters flowing from the different streets. Kingabwa, his neighbourhood, holds the record for flooding. One night, he and his family had been forced to leave their godforsaken house because they had been visited by the furious waters with nowhere to go because of a lack of gutters.

1PM. On this April afternoon, the unforgiving sun has stripped off. It can't be looked at. Water and tissues are bought and are then casually discarded after use, when everything is put in place to make some areas beautiful. Cars and other items born out of technology generate dust. Here, food is exposed, there, foul smells jump at the throat of passers-by; here, a pile of rubbish, there, fish is being fried. Sékélé's rickshaw painted in the fading national colours – red, blue and yellow, and on which are written the nickname of Equipe-epola-te and his phone number, no longer looks new. Almost a rectangular shape, 2m x 1, it carries a lot of goods: bags of rice, frozen fish, bags of maize, cassava, bananas. He is a "clean and civilised" rickshaw man; he doesn't carry things like rubbish. With him, it is clean goods only.

He wants to earn his money in an honest manner. He's not like most of the idle young men betting on the Pari-Foot with meagre sums in the hope of reaping huge sums of money. He doesn't want a life based on probabilities or statistics. Even if there is nothing wrong with dreaming – it was Martin Luther King who said, "I have a dream," both his feet are firmly planted on the ground. For someone who suffers from high blood pressure, without any buffer, his body and his heart give in easily to seduction. He won't be able to bear with psychic knocks and that's why he doesn't watch the games of his favourite team; he just hears the results. Surprise is his Achilles' heel.

The pilot Sékélé is behind his machine with his trousers rolled up to his knees. The rickshaw weighs about 950 kgs. Regardless, the face, the hands and the feet are determined to face up to this day, to that weight. The two women try to help him. The equal of Hercules sweats, the word of God is being accomplished. His whole body is at the mercy of the unforgiving and the ultra-violet rays of the sun. He is unrecognisable. Barefooted, his slippers somewhere in his rickshaw, he defies the mud, the sun, the broken bottles, the warm sand, the rubbish piles, the buses, the passers-by, the stagnant waters. He has 2,500 Francs, earned from his first trip, preciously stashed away in his pocket. He wants to earn more to guarantee the livelihood of his family. Jams however come to complicate the task. It becomes about trying to find a way among the buses and the motorcycles. Voices are raised with the drivers, the wewa, who've started growing in number in this mystery-town of more than ten million people. Sékélé lives in Kin la belle, Kin la poubelle, Kin Babel, in the Difficult Republic to Control, where everyone is a master in his own little corner.

"Move your stuff from here. This road is not for rickshaws!" An Esprit-de-mort driver throws at him.

Sékélé, who has lost his voice, makes a sign for him to jump with his bus dragging the spirit of death after it, and to go on his way.

"Look! Your money has fallen," the driver tells him.

Seeing nothing on the ground and having made sure that his little treasure is safely ensconced in the vault of his pocket, he turns towards the driver, places his finger on his temple before removing it whilst muttering some words. The driver is aware of the insult and throws back at him.

"Mutu'a pusu! Is it me? Today is the first. It's your problem if you don't keep your wits about you. Keep on dreaming."

Sékélé doesn't want to hear a word.

"Go, have fun with your father if he's alive, or with your mother. You don't know me. Look at this upstart! Look at this person! Instead of dealing with his steering wheel, he sees nothing better than to challenge me in the middle of the road. Ah, God of Sékélé, when I still was!"

The road breathes again. The driver starts his engine and laughs, happy to have done well with his joke.

The way to go becomes shorter and shorter. Sékélé keeps his spirits up. Today belongs to him and things are looking good. He is on his fourth trip and he has already earned a well-deserved 2,500 Francs, a fruit of a hard labour. He mentally does his calculations: 500 Francs for the bribe of the policemen, 500 Francs for the rice and beans taken on credit from the woman at the restaurant without forgetting the 150 Francs for the sachets of water. That is not taking into account what the two women will pay, added to that, another last trip, and there would be something to put under one's teeth this evening.

He constantly thinks about his little family left at home without any money. He is tired, but he carries on nonetheless. He pushes the rickshaw, pushes again. He needs to go uphill and a pothole has formed on the road which the authorities have trouble repairing. The sinews on his hands, arms, and on the muscles of his legs are visible. Another push! Two, three, he pushes, tries to shake it, pushes again, pulls, raises there and lowers here, and finally, it is done. It was the last trial and he's passed it, the brave one. They are a few metres away from the market where he needs to drop the goods of the two women. He has to breathe. Out of breath, he rests for a moment, to catch his breath. He passes a finger on his forehead to wipe the sweat off his face.

Something vibrates in the pocket of his trousers, then a loud ringtone reaches his eardrums. He takes it out, and checks the time. It is a message, from an unknown number. He reads it, doesn't see it well however, and understands nothing.

"Maman, please read this for me. What are they saying? It's the people from the network, hein?"

"It's from someone called Sedi."

"OK. It's a younger brother from my neighbourhood. He sells phone credits in front of my house. What does he say?"

"He wrote, 'Vieux, Maman Mampasi, your wife and your son Samy have been flattened by an Esprit-de-mort about 30 minutes ago. They have been taken to the hospital in a critical state. Sender 0813209168. Sent 01st, April 2016 at 3:30.'

The news fell on his ears the way the nuclear bombs fell on Hiroshima and Nagasaki. He thinks it is a dream, blood flows in his body at a quicker pace, adrenaline rises, cold sweats soak him, he tries to think.

When? How? Why? He watches the sky, he sees everything in black, like a thousand stars. Darkness falls on him. He is on the ground. A crowd of people quickly gathers around him, the way flies surround a mango. Among the crowd, there was the driver of Esprit-de-mort smirking, with his hands on his hips.

5:15PM. A long corridor, which seems to stretch endlessly. Right at the bottom, on the right, there is a room. In that room, there are four beds, and in the one that is by the door, there is a man. He is lying down as if he is dead. A needle pierces his right arm. He is on a drip. A nurse tries to take his blood pressure. The inopportune visitor in that bed is Sékélé. He can barely open his eyes. He's persecuted by the world, by the year, the month, the week, the day, this date. By his side, stand two people, his wife and his son, they are well apart from the fact that hunger is gnawing at their insides. They arrived late because they thought that it was a joke, but it is true. They are sad to see their man in that state.

Some distance away, a jubilant crowd, attracting a deafening noise, floods the street and creates an even bigger jam. The steps of this swarm of excited people are rhythmed by a song taken up and sung by everyone: men and women, young and old. Young people are at the head of this human train, the old and the mothers occupy the bottom. In this unspeakable heat and with quite a few of them in black and abhorring sunglasses, they must be sweating buckets. A few of them are more joyous than sad. The chorus of the song is "Fool-foul". The melody of a famous Congolese singer has been used for the chorus.

A few metres from there, a car pretending to be a limousine, rings out the signal of its departure through a siren. Going forth, the crowd gets added to by people in quest of adventures. In the middle of that crowd, a well-decorated rickshaw is pushed by a man dressed in white. At the head of the crowd, a beautiful coffin, which young people stoned on weed, shake, sometimes slowly, sometimes faster.

"Where to, Papa?" An onlooker asked.

"Between Earth-and-Heaven, Necropolis."

"Who's bitten the dust?"

"A man. Sékélé is his name."

"What did he die of?"

"April's Foul."

Decisive Moments

Idza Luhumyo

"To me, photography is the simultaneous recognition, in a fraction of a second, of the significance of an event." Henri Cartier-Bresson

(Notes on the photograph of a woman in a black dress, sitting in the sun)

The first time I met her, she was sitting outside her house on a stool, directly under the sun. It was such a peculiar place for a person to sit that I immediately concluded that she was doing this for medicinal reasons.

She had just finished reading the newspaper and was thinking on it.

She said to me: "I don't make many rules about life. I believe that an artist's life cannot be planned. I think it is supposed to be made to work with whatever comes along. But this one rule I have: I take time to slowly and carefully think about the things I read – this is my way of laying my claim on them, my way of making the things I read my very own."

I

The call-out had been clear: "Send us two of your best photographs and win a fully sponsored trip to an East African island of your choice."

The requirements of the call-out had been equally clear: be a woman who took her own photographs, be a woman who was African and lived in Africa, be a woman who had African parents.

There was no choice for her to make. For her, it had been and would always be Zanzibar.

Zanzibar: black coast, spice coast.

Zanzibar: the place where she had dispersed her husband's ashes after keeping the urn on a shelf in what had been their bedroom together, and then what later became her bedroom alone when she moved to a house closer to the ocean.

The urn was a way of keeping him close to her in death — just as he had been in life.

She had stayed with the ashes for a little over ten years. There was that peculiar comfort she derived from keeping his ashes within easy reach. Keeping his ashes close to her meant that he still kept on living; that he was not really dead.

It meant that he was "living-dead": a concept she'd once drummed into her primary-school students a long time ago while teaching the subject 'History'. A *History* with a capital "H", a *History* sandwiched between Geography and Civics by the curriculum planners, a *History* that was eventually yanked away from her when the school administration found her teaching things that did not appear on the Table of Contents of Malkiat Singh's History books.

And yet it was not the urn that posed a problem for her husband's people. It was the ashes that scared them. What kind of things did a woman do with a man's ashes in her bedroom? And not just any woman, but a woman who was never seen in anything but black clothes — a woman who always kept her hair covered and arranged on top of her head like a crown. And they wondered what kind of man their brother had become, forming his hands around a pen to write a will "asking" for his body to not only be cremated but for his ashes to be dispersed into the ocean by this woman he had insisted on calling his "wife" against the blessing of his fathers?

She had been a resolutely quiet wife, warding off children as one does evil spirits. Already there were rumors of a head full of *mvi* (at thirty years old!) wafting back to the village and so it was only inevitable that hatred for her, from her husband's people, would eventually follow. Yet this did nothing to her spirit. She handled the hatred the way she handled other inconveniences of her life: a carefully-cultivated indifference.

II

It is a little after midday. She finds it too hot for shoes. She finds it too hot to walk barefoot.

Compromising, she puts on her sandals and walks towards the back of the house, slicing through the afternoon silence. She walks past her dog Tunda who is lying on his favorite place, a patch of grass next to the bougainvillea plant.

She is already moving away from the confines of the present and stepping into the territory of the past. She finds that the past has come calling in the form of a newspaper call-out.

At the back of the compound she fumbles under the roof and finds a key holder with two keys.

She remembers how they'd built this shed together years ago, when the property on which it stands had only been a farm they worked on with their own hands, planting vegetables for consumption and for sale. And when the days got too hot for them to keep tilling the land, they would seek respite from the sun in this shed.

But that was then. Now, she uses it as a structure to keep the past under lock and key.

She opens the door to the shed and remembers the rampage she'd gone on after Tunje died, burning with fury that he had left her all alone in the world. She recalls how this rage had driven her into bundling up Tunde's things into boxes and sacks and then dragging them to the shed. And this is where his things remained for years and years, away from the main house where they only reminded her of her pain. But now, failing to keep up her indifference any longer, and failing to prevent the past from catching up with her, she opens the door into the shed.

(Notes on the photograph of a woman in a black headscarf, staring intently at a photograph)

There are times I would find her covered in dust, sneezing her way through old photo albums.

Once, after I had done some clicking away, she looked at me and said: "It was rage, first at Tunje's death, and then at death in general, that made me bring these photo albums here. And now, after all these years, I am surprised to find the rage I felt all those years ago still intact."

III

She finds a photograph that stills her.

She gets up and closes the window, suddenly aware of a slight chill on her skin.

She finds a chair.

She thinks of these things: she's nearing sixty years. She has given up coffee. Grudges. Salt. Sugar. She has finally come to understand loss.

And yet.

She finds that she is still a woman who can be completely unraveled by a photograph.

A memory comes from wherever memories come: This used to be her favourite photograph.

It hits her: This used to be her favourite photograph.

This used to be her favorite photograph.

How could she have forgotten about it?

She stares at it for a long, long time. Then she flips it, looking for any writings. She finds none.

It is incredible, she thinks, that she remembers nothing. She now begins to understand that it's possible for someone to completely forget about things that they once loved furiously.

She finds herself in some kind of panic, as if something is amiss in her, as if something in her life goes unaccounted for.

She slowly looks around her, and then finally at herself, as if meeting herself anew.

She is suddenly not sure what to trust and what not to trust. What else is she forgetting, she wonders?

She goes back to the photograph at hand. It is desaturated, with enough color to escape the "black and white" category, but not enough of it to be fully embraced by the "color" category. It is grainy and textured, inviting those who gaze upon it to pass their hands over it.

She studies it. It is late afternoon in the photograph. She can tell because of the slant of the light. She has always known her way around light, which is the only reason she picked up the camera thirty-three years ago. Tunje used to call her "the reader of light".

Another memory floats to her: this is where she picked up her habit of partly drawn curtains.

There is an open window in the background of the photograph. A sliver of bright light can be seen flowing into the room and illuminating the contents of the bed like some kind of torch.

A photograph inventory:

A blue, black *leso* that doubles up as a towel. Its twin folded next to it. A flowery dress used as a nightdress.

Bits and pieces of undecipherable clothes, unrecognisable for what each is, able only to be made sense of as a collective "clothes".

The clothes belonged to her grandmother, her father's mother.

Another memory:

She remembers the day they bundled up her grandmother in the neighbour's pick-up truck and sped off towards Coast General Hospital.

And now the memories come quicker, as if tripping over themselves, as if delighted to be let out of the confines of the past to take up their rightful space in this present.

First, she remembers how her grandmother screamed as they were carrying her towards the pick-up truck, protesting against what she insisted was "white people's medicine".

Then she remembers how her mother and aunt had still persisted, carrying her grandmother throughout the resistance, losing *lesos* and slippers in the process.

She also remembers how her grandmother had kicked her feet, causing her *leso* to fall off her waist, and exposing her *hando*. She remembers how her grandmother had yanked off her waist beads and how the beads had gone under the sofa and the beds and then, finally, to her and her siblings' surprise, yanked off her head wrap and exposing hair that nobody had ever seen. Black kinky hair laid close to the scalp in cornrows.

The pick-up truck then sped off to the hospital.

And then the decisive moment: she had picked up her grandmother's scarf. She had tied it on her hair and then from that day, refused to ever remove it. She also refused to remove from her head many other scarves that she would later buy for herself. And along the way, when she came to be known as the girl who always had a head scarf, she found out that people were very nervous around people who kept their hair covered. In this way, she found herself retreating more and more into herself.

The window into her memory opens wider.

She now remembers that after her mother and aunt had taken her grandmother to the hospital, she had walked into the room her grandmother used to sleep in and started to take pictures, as if instinctively knowing that when they brought her from the hospital, it would be in a white bundle, escorted by wailing women who were dressed in matching *kishutus*, women who smelt of tobacco and coconut oil, women who had been born already knowing the melody to funeral songs in their hearts.

As is the nature of memory, she does not remember the events that immediately came after the funeral. Instead, her memory carries her to another moment; another decisive moment. She remembers how her aunt had made her sit next to three of her cousins and then narrated to them the life story of her grandmother.

First, that her grandmother had only worn black cotton dresses. And then this: that she always kept her hair covered under black scarves, making herself even blacker in a household that was full of people with light skins.

Her grandmother's father had worked for a long time as a faithful servant in a Swahili household. And as a result of his dedication, he had been allowed to bring his daughter to the household so that she could get to grow up in a good Muslim household.

But as soon as the daughter got to Majengo Mapya, a son of the house liked her, got her pregnant and saw no problem in marrying her. Two children later, she got tired of the insults that would get passed over her head because of the colour of her skin and her tough *kipilipili* hair.

She had become tired of being called a *Mnyika*, a woman who belonged to a community of rat-eaters and people-eaters, a *Mshenzi* who knew no God and had no faith.

So she looked for a *leso*, threw a few clothes in, made two knots, found Swaleh — her husband — seated on the verandah outside the house and said to him: "Please, give me my divorce."

Back to her father's land, her *talaka* having been given to her, she said to whoever would listen: "I will always wear black clothes — now that they insulted me for being black."

And whenever she got questions about the two children she had left behind when she got her divorce, she would sigh and say that her children had been favored with light skins and that would be enough to guarantee them much easier lives than she could ever give them.

Right now, as she looks at the photograph, she remembers that many, many years after her grandmother had died, she had been sitting next to a friend in the dark room, watching photographs take shape. And when the one she is looking at now emerged, she began crying, explaining through her tears that this was the only photograph she had of her grandmother.

Her friend, not seeing anyone in the picture and not understanding, frowned, and said: "There is no one in that picture, Salame."

But Salame had only laughed, explaining that her grandmother had been famously suspicious of photographs. She had been a woman who had been happy to live her entire life without any form of pinning down.

But here in this photograph, Salame explained to her friend in that dark room, her grandmother was present — even in her absence. Especially in her absence.

She was present in the clothes and present in the room, present in the photograph and present in the shed.

Her grandmother had come to her from beyond the grave like a wave: her gait, her manner of speaking, her birdlike enterprise, her quietness, the smell of the tobacco she smoked — even the slipperiness of the coconut oil she smeared on her skin.

And as she now looks at the photograph, tracing her hand all over it, she feels like she has finally come full circle. She is finally full: a woman complete with her memories. To be human, she feels, would be an incomplete experience without easy access to her memories.

(Notes on the photograph of a woman bent over a photo album with a pair of glasses hanging on the bridge of her nose)

The last time I visit her before I leave, she tells me that it took her a whole month to work through her old work, another month to choose one photograph, and then another month to blow on her old camera, to put the camera around her neck and to press her thumb — an old habit — on the shutter.

She tells me that the first photograph she took is of her dog Tunda, settled into his favorite place near the bougainvillea flowers.

She said to me: "It took me seventeen years to start taking photographs again. And by the time I decided to bring my photo albums into the house again, I knew that I had already won the contest, whichever way it went."

Duiweltjie

Megan Ross

Self-tan is expensive as fuck. It's the night before the scout's coming and I'm marching through SPAR, trying to find the right stuff. Tropitone is a great brand, but it wasn't until I made friends with the older girls that I realized you never use one brand alone. You've got to mix it up. You see, you can't just slap on the stuff and hope it's going to look good. At Copacabana we pride ourselves on looking natural. There's no fake titties or siff orange tans here. You can stuff off to Miami Beach if that's what you want. Ja: don't know who you've been talking to but none of those birds are real. You really think tits stay that perky when you're thirty? Dream on, bud.

So back to the tanner: you have to buy two bottles — one a shade darker than your skin, and one a shade lighter. You're never going to find the right match so the trick is to take the shit home, squeeze a little out both tubes and mix it in a little bakkie. Don't use a wooden spoon, a tablespoon works best. Imagine you're folding in the mixtures, like when you bake a cake. Ja, you've got it. So you fold it in, first the light and then add tablespoons of the dark until you've got a close enough mix to your own colour. No, you don't want to look dark. That's not the point. If the okes want black chicks they'll go to a black fucking club.

We *want* to look like white girls, okay? Not coloured, white.

No, I don't think there's anything wrong with what I've just said. People have preferences, okay? These guys don't come in here because they've been forced; this is a *pleasure* thing. You've got to make them feel good. And they want what they want. Same as if you like your eggs hard boiled or soft. You can't help what you like and you're not going to enjoy what you don't. So.

Please stop interrupting me. I can't get my story straight if you keep doing that.

Okay, so you spoon dollops of darker tanner into the lighter one, until you've got this golden bronzy mixture. Now that is what you're after: you want to look like the golden Oscar statue version of yourself, not like a darkie. When it looks like your own skin but glittery, that's when it's perfect. Lots of the girls use those spray machines: Paula got a nice second hand one from a church bazaar but I've realized I can't really get the nooks and crannies like I can with my fingers. I mean, I do some pretty wide pliés on stage: ain't no chance I'm getting away with a half job, if you know what I'm saying.

I usually leave it until the night before so my tan is fresh as death. That's from a Lana Del Rey song, you like her? Oh ja, she's amazing! I do my eyes just like hers: with that sixties flick and that dark liner right to the corner. The guys really go for it: they think it's exotic or something but I want to tell them: your mothers wore it just like that in the sixties. But I don't. They've all got mommy issues but you're not going to be getting any tips by telling them that.

I do a dance to this one Lana Del Rey song, that one? Uhm, West Coast, ja, West Coast.

If you're not drinking, then you're not playing. Ja, she is beautiful. Her music videos are so deep, like, she doesn't do much choreography but that's okay because her voice is practically the most beautiful thing I have ever heard.

I have six outfits.

Some of the girls have more but they've been working longer and they can afford to splash out. I like to rotate during my shift, so I'm always looking kinda different for my numbers. Some of the other girls just change their boas or a bikini but I go all out: I've hand-stitched sequins to every bikini and lined them with gold fabric so if my top comes off during the act it catches the light whichever side it lands.

But then it's back to me. Eyes here, boys: I'm the main attraction.

There's something about me. I've heard all the guys say it. I'm mysterious, you know. I've got that dark-horse thing going. Eileen hated that, when I first started. She said it's only because I'm young that they like me.

That bitch.

She is so jealous of me. Just because my hair's naturally dark and my eyes are really green; she's worn contacts since the get go and she can't afford to wear them anymore because they make her eyes itch; and nobody wants a girl who's half crying on stage cause her eyes are itching, makes the customers feel funny. She's back to brown. Despite not being the prettiest girl, she gets a fair amount of shouting when she comes on stage. But you know what they say, if it's not in the looks, it's in the broeks, and oh my word, does she like to do the upside-down splits.

She uses the pole a lot, whereas I choose to use my space. I move, you see. I'm a dancer, not a stripper. I don't just spin around a stupid fireman effort like a child. Eileen, though, she uses that pole like a crutch; spinning and climbing like a monkey. Legs wide open and all, which is pretty disgusting because she has no qualms showing the guys her fanny.

I'm classier than that.

I insisted, when I signed. No fanny. I don't mind showing my titties every now and then, because that can be really artistic in a Lana kinda way.

But not my front.

Yes — my bottoms are small but the most I'll do is, like, a slight G-string action. But I turn around quickly! Don't want my clients thinking that's what I'm all about; because I'm definitely not. I'm the only real dancer here, the only trained one. Not one of these chicks knows a real step or anything. I'm classically trained, did I tell you that? Royal Academy of Ballet. The patron is the King of England, or, or something. How smart is that?

I did years of it. My mother made me. At first I hated it. But I was good. Damn good. And then I started Modern, and Spanish, and soon I was doing all the fucking classes you could do at that school. Teachers hated me but the examiners? They passed me with flying colours, darling. Honours every *fucking* time. Dancing was always my favourite thing. I wasn't bad at sport but when it came to the music, wow, I just came alive, you know? Like something deep in me moved of its own accord.

Like something in me bloomed.

That's where I got my name actually. Rose. From the feeling I get when I'm dancing. Starts when the music begins, like this little itch is being scratched in my heart, and all of a sudden I'm petals falling to the ground: dark and red like something painful. Like something beautiful.

My dad used to call me Duiweltjie. My little devil thorn, he'd say, tousling my hair. That's before he left us for that whore in Amalinda. Started up a second family like it wasn't even a thing. Like me and my sister and Mommy didn't even exist. He tried to keep in contact but I just couldn't stomach him after his son was born. Acted like we were brother and sister. *Brother and sister?* With a sixteen year gap?

Hells no.

He owns a body shop on the Quigney, close to work, actually. Some of the guys come to the club after hours, when the lights are dimmed and only the stage is lit and the air snaps like an alligator or a Lycra leotard between your fingers. When he heard I was dancing there he just about flipped his lid. I was in real kak with my boss, the one time, because he rocked up drunk and tried to drag me off the stage, just when I was starting my Alejandro routine. You know that song? Gaga? It's glorious. When I first saw the video I cried: she's so beautiful and she knows exactly how to move her body to make you feel something. Never mind the music. I knew I had to dance to that song the second I watched that video, and I loved doing that routine, every time.

But that night that my dad came? All bullish and thinking he can boss me around and shit? Like time hasn't passed and he didn't abandon me for a spitty baby and a gross wife with ankle sores and a muffin top? Yoh, the in*jus*tice.

'But my Duiweltjie,' he went on, pleading with me, while the song is still going and all the men are looking on like this old man is my pervert-boyfriend and not my stupid father. Because that's a problem, you see: the guys can't be thinking that I have a boyfriend. It ruins my whole act. I am untouchable: I am Rose, she of the petals and the dark centre and the cluster of bloody thorns dancing all around my body. Now if I'm supposed to be so untouchable, I can't exactly have this fat, old dude looking like he owns me, you see.

Sure, caused a bit of a stir, and one or two of the guys got up to say something, but I managed to signal to Andrew to get Teneille on stage, and the guys soon forgot about what happened when she dropped her panties after two twirls. But did I tear a strip off my father? Jesus. The man hasn't bothered me since. He was pathetic, really, couldn't see that I'm grown up and I've left his ugly ass behind. The guys at the body shop tease him about it. They vloek him, in their overalls, laughing with their spray masks and canisters of white and green.

I don't need a daddy anymore, I told him, pushing his ham-like shoulders out the side door. You left a long, long time ago, don't come back here with stories. I'm done. He went on about the guys at his body shop:

My precious, the boys talk about you all the time. What about me? How are they going to respect the boss-man when his daughter's just a stripper down the road?

Yoh, now that's when I lost it. He was really drunk at this stage, you see, the brandy had most definitely kicked in for-real, and so I gave him the boot — literally — and he fell against the outside wall, crumpling into a sorrowful heap.

I don't have time for this; I told him, trying to ignore the ugly, niggling feeling that had suddenly started somewhere down in my solar plexus. I don't need this *kak* from a man who abandoned me years ago.

And I meant it, you see. Sure, the boys are talking, but I'm not ashamed of being a dancer. I'm the best there is this side of the Buffalo River. Ain't nobody with my feet, or my eyes, or my grace. You see it in the guys' faces: something softens when I begin, as if I'm really reaching the goodness inside of them; that last little inkling of something innocent: I pluck it like a cord.

I'm not an ordinary woman, you see. I'm the kind great men write about and sorrowful men sing to. I could've been Chris de Burgh's Lady in Red, or Michael Jackson's Billie Jean. Either one. I've just got that *thing*, you see. That quality that's more than a great ass or a really mean grand battement. The X Factor. I've got the Bridge of Sighs in the arch of my foot and Paris all around my ankles. I can be as ordinary as they come one day and hot-as-shit the next. Chameleon — that's what Andrew said I am. Men always try to name us, you noticed that? First I'm a thorn, and then I'm a bug. That's why I renamed myself. On the stage. Named myself after the prettiest flower there is. Rose Rose Rose.

Men are all really just little boys, you see. They grow big and bold and into these hairy bodies that serve them well when they're hiding from their feelings, which is most of the time. But give them something real; an experience that is *definitive*, you know, childbirth, labour, divorce, *love*, and they crumble to hell and weep for their mothers.

It's women who do the real growing. Year after year our souls expand, taking on all that we go through, swallowing up and feeding the flowers inside of us. It doesn't look like it but we are powerful. I see it when I'm on stage and enthralling every little boy inside the room.

All just looking for their mommies, every single one.

Thing is, after my dad left, I had to do a little regrouping. Had to make myself seem untouchable, again, not virginal — that's Saskia's groove, not mine — but so dark and far away, like a dream they can't quite fathom; a memory both bad and good. I had to become myself, again.

See, dancing's like going window shopping. Sure, you can look. But you can't touch. Never, ever, ever. Not even the ugly broads with the varicose veins hiding under their Spanx. We're not that kind of club.

There's a scout coming from the States. He's looking for dancers to take back to LA, where he's got dance instructors and a mansion of a house and a whole lot of contacts in the industry. I'm going to dance for J.Lo! I'm going to be on TV. Maybe, and this might be a long shot but I'm prepared to work hard: we'll be in the movies.

Eileen says it's fishy. But Eileen is a fat bitch with no fucking clue about anything. Thinks just because she went to tech she has a flying chance of making it out of here. But she's wrong, and I'll show her. Besides, the shit she said was disgusting. Porn rings, home-made videos. The kind of shit they film on cell phones and then pay you nothing for. Doesn't even sound real. And besides, I'm a dancer, not a stripper. I'm not going to do porn — that was never the point to any of this.

Andrew isn't happy about it. Says the scout is coming to steal his girls even though he's already ordered some Johnny Walker Blue and made Patricia clean his fancy glasses. Wants to impress the guy but then stop us from getting opportunities? Doesn't work like that, bud. I've already planned my outfit: been saving a little for new fabric, and Bessie's just got in this beautiful bale of deep pink stretch. I got Gloria to stitch it together: usually I do it myself but this time I wanted the lining done perfect, and she's got an over locker so she can do it really neat.

It's just a bit of cam work, he said. Really private too: I've got my own channel and you can only view it if you sign up. And pay. It's decent pay straight into my account. After his cut, though. Obviously. Guy's got to eat too. Okay, it's not always fun. There's some real creeps and I have to spend time texting them, too.

But it's one step closer to the dream. One little rung up the ladder.

I'm struggling to get my pay. I'm fighting with the boss man now, and Andrew doesn't want anything to do with me since the guys all know what I'm doing after hours. It's not what I bargained for. None of it is. I thought getting scouted meant a ticket to America. I thought it meant the American fucking dream. Blue stripes and red stars and bikinis on the beach.

There's another guy, though. Says I'll have my own room. He'll pay for my ticket and everything: visas will get sorted out too. It sounds tempting. I'll see how it pans out.

It's hard, here. People aren't as friendly as they seem on TV. And I have a lot of cam work to do before they let me do anything on stage. There's an audition I want to go to; for a back up gig. I'm going to try get the bus there, as soon as I can figure out the routes. We don't have busses like this in South Africa. There isn't a chance I'd know how to use these back home.

He hit me. I have a bruised lip and a funny mark across my nose but it's okay, they'll cover it up in makeup tomorrow. I'm doing my first group act. It's not the work I wanted to do, but it'll pay the bills that keep piling up here and this way I can make something towards my dreams. I can stash it away. Dollars to Rands, Rands to Dollars. I can't stop doing the conversions in my head. Backwards and forwards. I'm calculating sums more than I ever have. I'm calculating dates: I had my period on the fourth. It's been thirty-five days. Am I just late? And they all use condoms, I've been assured.

I'll be protected.

I'm leaving. I have to. They've taken me for tests but they won't let me see the results. I have no say in anything. I told the boss man and he just about flipped. Told me to leave if I want, there'll be others. I could barely afford the ticket, but there's another girl in the house — a Mexican girl — and she leant me some cash when I promised I'd pay it back soon as I'm home.

It's too late for the pills. I go to the state hospital, for a procedure that's quick and clean. I'm all empty now. I feel strange. My father keeps calling: he heard I'm back and he wants to help. Seems everyone knows what happened over there. I haven't told anyone but the industry is small. People talk.

I am not your Duiweltjie, I told him. Leave me be. I am no one and nobody's. Not the thorn in your side, not the prickling beneath your feet. I am just my own. I am Rose. Rose of the glitter and the breasts and the shiny pole in the centre of the stage. I am petals falling gracefully to the ground, swept up in my own winds, flawless as a diamond.

Yes, I am Rose. I am I am I am.

I get my cards read. By this old coloured woman on the beach front. It's an old pack. Worn around the edges. Makes me trust her somewhat. If she believes, I believe. Five of Cups. Means disappointment, apparently. The disappointment is a disappointment. I wanted something bright: I wanted hope.

I dismiss the cards. Yes, I'm dancing at Sugar Shack. But what's your point? I'm only doing it to save and when I've got enough money I'm buying a ticket to Jozi because that's where all the real stuff is happening. None of this small-town shit for me. No Sirree. I am going to get out if it's the last thing I do.

Even if it kills me.

Free fall

Praise Nabimanya

There are things my mother did not understand. Like the fact that I was past the point of caring whether they gave my aunt a goat as a reward for helping preserve my virginity, or about my reputation being tarnished, resulting in my father, mother and entire household becoming fodder for the village gossip.

I had never been lucky in love. I had tried, of course, only as much as a girl can, to make myself marriageable. I had learnt cooking; after all, the way to a man's heart is through his stomach. So it was beans, potatoes (both Irish and sweet), yams, luwombo (a delicacy made by steaming food in special banana leaves), all kinds of greens that men ate, even when for a long time I did not know what they were for, until my aunt explained when I was of reasonable age that they gave men "power". Basically, everything that was edible in my village, you name it, I cooked. I learnt scrubbing and cleaning, weeding around the house, the art of organising a homestead. I tilled the land without tiring. My mother never left me behind whenever she went to the gardens.

I was nineteen when I had my first suitor, Jamos. We had grown up together as neighbours. We had played house together right from when we were kids. Most of the households would be up by 5am. The men and boys would take the cows and goats to graze and the girls would prepare their breakfast, which had to be ready by 7am, so that the boys would not be late for school. We would also make sure their lunch was ready by 1pm, when they came back from school ready to join the men in the grazing fields.

It was only inevitable that Jamos and my friendship would grow into something more.

I loved him.

*

We had been together at the village well when Jamos first complained of a slight stomach ache. We had both dismissed it as nothing but a little food poisoning.

What we both took as a small sickness developed into a full-blown disease that had the man I loved wailing in pain for seven days until he succumbed.

Nothing could be done. Both the clinic medicine and the traditional herbs had not helped ease the pain. I cried myself to sleep for three months.

When I had no suitors after that. I started thinking I was cursed. As the years went by and the villagers talked, I lost all hope of ever having a family of my own, let alone getting married. And there I was, 37 years old and still a spinster. Girls that had been born when I was grown up were already nursing their third-born babies.

Then I had finally found a man willing to marry me.

*

My mother did not understand. Just the last Sunday evening she had called me, her voice piercing with urgency, "Eva."

"Yes, Mukyala," I replied, running to her room.

"Sit here," she said, patting the place next to her on the bed. "I want you to listen, and listen carefully."

I sat hastily, very curious.

"Today after church, your aunt Mabel pulled me aside and told me some very disturbing things. It's not that I believe them, of course, but I want you to tell me the truth."

"Mukyala, what is it?" I asked.

"The women are moving around with rumours that you are sleeping with Musa," she said, closing her eyes. "Is it true?"

My heart beating fast, I touched her arm and shook my head.

I lied to my mother.

I totally had no qualms about it though. I did not see it as wrong to have sex with the man that was going to marry me. I just knew Mukyala would rip out her own heart if she had even a hint that those speculations could be carrying a little grain of truth.

She looked at me, her hands squeezing mine emphatically.

"Okay, I believe you. Not that I doubted your innocence. I just wanted to make sure. You know how wrong it is. And you know how people will take up the least bit of smoke and make it into a full blaze. Do not visit Musa again. Even if it's during the day. People will talk," she said. "I will not have them thinking that my only daughter is making herself available as a cheap whore before all the sacrifices are fully made."

"Of course, Mother. I will not go to his house again," I added.

My mother was the woman that other women brought their girls to for proper counselling before they got married.

So it was suitable that I lied to her about Musa.

*

Musa, still young at 46, had been widowed six months before. His wife had died in childbirth, leaving him with a crying baby and three young children to look after. His sister had looked after them till she could not any more. Her husband had complained she was neglecting her own marital home.

One evening, Musa and my father had been seated at the local bar drinking gin and smoking pipe tobacco when it suddenly occurred to my father that I could help look after Musa's children, take on after his sister. By a stroke of luck, Musa actually considered it and decided to give it a shot. My father must have been elated at the prospect because discussions were made and the match was made, just like that.

I still remember with joy in my father's voice when he gave me the news two days later.

"My child, I have finally got you a man," he said happily.

"Eeh! Father, what do you mean?" I asked.

"Look." He was grinning. "It is my responsibility to make sure you're looked after. You're my daughter. Musa is a very good man. He has resources. He will look after you. His children are young. They will not stress you."

"But are you sure? I mean, is that what Musa really wants?" I asked, bewildered.

"I have already talked to Mukyala and she is okay with it, very happy for you. All that's left is just the formal arrangements. I'm meeting with your uncles this evening to discuss matters."

Two weeks and four heads of cattle later, I was engaged to Musa Batambara.

Mukyala and my aunt Mable were brimming with joy. My mother because finally people were going to stop saying she had raised her daughter wrong and Mable mostly because she was looking forward to receiving a goat for carrying out her duties to perfection.

My Musa was quite a catch. His herd of cattle was large, he was sturdy and tall, his father had been the LC1 chief, and he had a three-year church school certificate in his CV. Sometimes I thought giving my body to such a man, especially given my circumstances, was something God would be willing to forgive.

Mukyala did not understand this.

After making love (he did not call it that but I liked to think it was), he used to kick the coarse covers of his wooden bed to the floor and lie on the bed chuckling loudly, then he would talk to himself quietly, as one praying. It is the only thing about him that scared me.

I liked him and how he made me feel and I liked the covetous looks of all the village girls when they looked at me – girls who used to think me ugly and cursed.

Four weeks to the wedding, every morning and evening, the married women led by my aunt would gather at the bridal hut where I was staying. I would strip naked and they would bathe me in fresh milk mixed with cleansing herbs. Then they would smear my whole body with scented "shanti", Vaseline blended with cow ghee, and bring me greens and meat to eat and bitter herbs to drink. Their words of caution daily droned in my ears, till I could recite each one off my head.

"Men speak once and you hear twice, Eva."

"Your role as a woman is to look after your man and your children, Eva."

"Never talk back to your man, girl."

They considered me equipped with all the details of the marriage bed. Then they would leave and check on me in several intervals to see that I was drinking and eating as I was supposed to.

*

It was two nights to the wedding when Musa sneaked into my hut, the one where I was being prepped into the perfect wife. It was almost midnight, the time when the night is darkest, quietest and the trees make shadows of devilish shapes — "Waringa", we called it. The women had all left. I was in that place between slumber and wakefulness when I heard a familiar "tap tap" on the hut's wooden door.

"Musa, it is late," I whispered, gingerly opening the door.

"I had to come, mukundwa, my beloved," he said. "We get married soon, after all."

"But the women, they could return any time."

"Please open up, my love. I'll be gone by the time they wake up."

"But, Musa, but..."

"Come on, I'll be fast," he said, his beseeching stamped by an intense seriousness in his eyes.

Even as I reasoned with him, I knew his pleading would eventually wear down my insistent refusal, as always. I slowly and quietly opened the door and let him in. He immediately reached for me and proceeded to claw at the blue lesu that was wrapped around my body. Seeing him fidgeting with it, I quickly untied the knot that held the lesu together on my right shoulder. Then we gave way to our baser wants, taking care to mute down the sounds and groans that could easily echo in the eerie silence of the night.

*

My eyes opened wearily toward daybreak. I looked around as I remembered the events of the previous night.

"Musa," I cried out, "it's time to go."

He didn't reply.

"Musa, Musa, wake up," I repeated.

Silence.

He must be dead asleep, I thought.

I moved my hands around to rouse him from sleep as my eyes got used to the early-morning light. I felt around only to touch something cold against my wrist. My first thoughts were that it was a snake!

I screamed and jumped off the bed naked, all the while shouting for him, wondering why he was not answering, if maybe he had already left. Immense panic gripped me as I rushed and threw open the small window made of wood to let in a little more light.

I turned around, looking for the hardened piece of wood I usually kept around in case of snakes. Turning towards the bed, I found myself staring into Musa's lifeless, wide-open eyes.

His dark skin was ashen, his black khaki trousers and grey shirt worn as if he was in a great hurry, the shirt unbuttoned and clinging to his cold, dead body.

"Musa," I said, my voice choking.

I could not find my voice.

I shouted and shook him again and again, more firmly. I shook his arms, his legs, his thighs, thumped his chest. Musa could not wake up.

I slid slowly on the floor. Strangely, my eyes were dry. I failed to cry. I must have sat there for hours, astounded, not willing to believe what was happening. Thoughts whirling in my mind. Thoughts of all the times I had cried and prayed to providence and God and any deity who cared to listen, to give me a husband, to deliver me from the curse and give me a family of my own.

Finally, I resolved to tell the only person I could: my mother.

She could tell something was wrong the moment she saw me, clad in only a lesu, eyes unfocused, standing in front of her house.

"What is it, Eva?"

I looked at her, unable to form words.

"Eva, what is it, you're scaring me."

"It's Musa."

She never believed it until I led her to the bridal hut and she saw Musa lying dead and stiff on the crumpled checkered bed sheets. I still remember her howling and flailing her arms about, making me explain over and over again what had happened.

"My God, a man in your bed! How could you do such an abominable and disgraceful thing?"

"You don't understand," I whispered.

"How many times did I warn you never to allow any man in your room before getting married to him? Didn't I caution you enough?

Oh Lord, where did I go wrong?" she cried.

I remained quiet.

My whole body was shaking. I could not see properly. I sank to the bed.

"Do you realise the scandal that you have caused? Your father will kill us both. What are we going to do now? What am I going to tell your father?" She paced around the small room, murmuring, carrying her arms on her head.

I was seated on the bed with Musa's body next to me.

It seemed hours later that Mukyala's voice broke through the haze.

"I have to tell your father," my mother said. "I'll have to find a way of breaking it to him."

It killed me to know she was ultimately trying to find ways of shielding me from the mess I had created.

"Stay here," she said. "Your father is over at your uncle's discussing the final wedding plans." She shook her head at the irony of it. "I'll go tell him. Just try to stay calm. I'll come back and find you."

Injeri River was just a ten-minute walk from my home. I cannot count how many times I had been there with Mukyala to wash clothes and fetch water whenever the well dried up. It was early morning so the possibility of finding the village women doing their laundry like we had often done was almost zero — most of them went down to the river in the afternoon hours, because mornings were spent doing other house chores and gardening before the sun became too hot.

My mind dazedly recalled the chitchat and the laughter of the women as they gathered around in groups, taking care of their families' dirty linen. The river had always been a haven, a place where they could rest from the demanding voices of their husbands and the backbreaking burden of looking after the homes in all ways. The sound of rushing water and the welcome happy chatter of the little children as they played was a comfort to the women. The river had always been a place where for a few times in our lives we could throw ourselves to complete abandonment and just be free.

Maybe that is why it was the first place to come to my mind.

I slowly made my way to the river bank and knelt right at the edge. The only thing that was real was the gripping pain I felt in my heart, the agony that was wrenching and tearing at me like little hooks of a harpoon.

Tears flooded my eyes but I could not bring myself to rub them away. I did not want to. I wept. I cried for Mukyala, who I knew would die from the grief of it all. I cried for my father and for my brothers. I cried for the children I would never have, I cried for Musa and for Jamos and for myself. I cried in despair and anguish because I had not been strong enough to beat the curse. I had finally surrendered and it had won. I would never get married. I would die an old spinster in my father's house, with no child of my own. I would be forgotten just months into the ground.

*

I heaved over, tears soaking my lesu. But Injeri was sympathising with me. She did not want me to cry. She flowed on, calling, willing to drown my tears and with them my pain. She had been my solace so many times and she was willing to be my solace forever.

There I squatted at the river's edge and stared into those dark waters. I was weeping loudly by now and the swirls of the cascading water were answering me back, beckoning me to join them on their peaceful journey.

I would find peace, wouldn't I?

Away from the hopelessness, the shame and the desperation that hung over me. I knew it was too late for me to hope for the happiness I had always craved. But at least I would not cry any more.

With that final thought, I held up my lesu and plunged into the river.

Grey Love

Jude Mutuma

Friday evenings reminded you of a previous life. They reminded you of loud, grungy music on high rooftops of buildings in the outskirts of Nairobi. They reminded you of cold evenings in warm places with strange boys whose breath smelt of cinnamon and whose names your lips could not remember the morning after. Friday nights reminded you of sex and sweat and the reckless bitter-sweetness of a life spent searching for escape, for meaning. They reminded you of a life before Rhosa.

That Friday did not hold memories. Instead, it bore arduous thoughts about the unspoken bleakness of tomorrows. Rhosa was right there in front of you. She was carrying a brown notebook and sat next to a lake just as the sun was rubbing its eyes. It was not a real lake. It was the large, polluted expanse of the Nairobi Dam. In the distance, large patches of pondweed stained its silvery surface with a hue of green. Farther ahead, a mustering of Marabou storks waded over the calm water, their long, skinny legs disturbing the smooth ripples.

She was wearing faded blue jeans and a grey T-shirt with the words "Love Me" inscribed on the front. Her hair was tied into tufts, kinky and stubborn against the gentle wind, and its blackness complemented her dark, supple skin. You were standing right behind her, wearing that blue dress Papa got you when you turned eighteen. It was sleeveless, a shy blue, the kind of dress that dances in the wind. It contrasted beautifully with your bright-red lipstick. You had never really liked the dress. But you were not wearing it for you. You were wearing it for her. Rhosa took out a red pencil from the left back pocket of her jeans and scribbled on a blank page near the middle of the notebook:

Rhosa & Lisa

Forever

She tore the page off and threw it in the lake. You watched as water hovered over scribbled lines — like floating dreams — on a crumpled sheet of paper. She asked you to listen to the silent throbbing of the water. You realised it was not really silent. With each ripple came a sound, soft and still, throb after throb. It was like the water had a heartbeat, a life of its own.

You gazed at the reflection of the setting sun on the face of the water. The lake was now a lazy mass of orange, stretching far and beyond, fading into the distance. Beyond the view of the lake, you could make out the rugged outline of a Nairobi city that was just beginning to come to life. A Nairobi whose days were cold and unnerving, but which suddenly bustled with a new energy after dark. Something about this view reminded you of Mother.

One time you asked Rhosa why she always came here. She poked your right cheek and said, "Release." You had grown accustomed to this routine. She liked to come here when she was like this; when the loudness of her own thoughts threatened to drive her insane. When she needed reassurance, needed to be reminded that she was not wrong. That this was not wrong.

She liked to be here, with you. The water, it soothed her. You soothed her. The wind came like a wisp, and it tickled your bare feet. She smiled — a half smile — and pointed to a grey cloud. In the cloud she claimed she saw your face. An image that had refused to leave her. She said the tiny scar just above your left eye made your face look like it had a story to tell. And you had this perpetual smirk on your face that seemed to tell everyone to go to hell. You both laughed.

You looked daintily at the cloud, searching for any semblance to your face. You found none. Instead, it reminded you of rising fumes of black smoke. You tried to shape the cloud into an image of Mother, smiling. Still there was nothing, only more black fumes, and a panicking realisation: You had forgotten what your mother looked like. You gazed even more deeply, desperate to mould the greyness into an image of something, of anything. Anything but the black fumes. Nothing came.

Rhosa turned around to ask you a question. "Do you believe in magic?"

"Almost." Almost. Such a shy word. You loved the taste of the word on your lips. It implied incompleteness; an existence that is not quite there yet. A presence that was not quite present. It was what you felt when you remembered Mother. You felt incomplete. You felt almost.

"Almost doesn't count," she said with a grin.

"Oh, *sawasawa.*"

"*Halafu?*"

"*Halafu* what?"

"Do you believe? Do you believe in magic?"

Silence.

You remembered watching the swishing of wands and chanting of "Patronus" spells and drinking of "Polyjuice" potions in the *Harry Potter* movies. But maybe magic was something far less complicated. The way she was smiling as she saw the sunset, you could tell that the sunset was her magic. You stood there gazing at the sky and you wondered whether your magic was standing right there in front of you, wearing a grey T-shirt and blue jeans.

You felt the wetness as it slithered on your face. A pain rose in your throat. You did not want her to see you like this. She stood up and faced you. Wiped the wet on your face using the back of her left hand. Asked you what was wrong, and you did not know how to tell her: Everything. Release. You could use some of that too. This was supposed to be goodbye. Your whole life had been a series of unwanted goodbyes, but at least this one would be on your terms. You needed to tell her that you could not do this. How could you do this? Every time you looked at her you felt this fire, burning fiery yellow in the black of night. But you are a girl, and she is a girl. This did not make sense. You loved her, yes, you loved her, and you wished that was all it took. But no. It could never amount to anything. Nothing is as simple as it should be. Everything is stuck under a blur. There is no black and white. The world is just a haze of grey.

You had planned to say goodbye. But things seldom go as planned.

"I love you."

"How much?" she said, smiling.

You told her, more than she could ever imagine.

"Do not tell me. Show me."

You held her cheeks in both of your hands and asked her to look in your eyes. You let her see fire in the pupils of your eyes and feel the heaviness of your breathing on her face. You told her that she is life. That she is the soothing relief of cool morning breeze in the blistering heat of January. She is the taste of sweet vanilla cream on your dry cracking lips after a long, hungry day. She is the smell of a flower; a rose, freshly plucked. She is the bridge to a John Legend song. Elegant. Cultured. A tad complicated. She is love and bliss and hope and fire, and perfection understated in words. You leant in and kissed her lips; a little kiss that lasted slightly longer than a second.

That, right there, that was magic.

*

It is another Friday night, and it tastes like bitter lemons. It holds the pain of having to remember the sadness carried in shared memories. It is here, this pain, floating in the uncomfortable talks and silences between a father and his daughter. You are driving to town in Papa's grey Volvo, Papa on the passenger seat, in the crisp winds of

Lang'ata Road at ten at night. It is the seventh day of August, 2015.

"Your brother called yesterday, *jioni*."

Papa's voice is raspier than when you last spoke. Old age is creeping up on him. Or maybe it is the cigarettes. He should slow down on the cigarettes.

"Cape Town seems to be treating him well. You should see the pictures he Whatsapped me. Who would have thought our Bahati could grow fat?"

The dry, empty laugh he lets out does nothing to conceal a hint of grief in his voice. You are not interested in this monologue. You turn your eyes from his face and stare at the winding road ahead.

"Do you miss him?" he asks.

"Of course," you say.

"He says he might come back this Christmas. He will apply for two weeks' leave."

You know. You have been talking to Bahati too. He has called you every week for the past nine months, ever since he left. He is not happy in South Africa. If they do not approve his leave request, he will quit his job.

There it is again, that silence that hangs heavily between the two of you. A silence that holds uncertainty. In such situations, Bahati was always the talkative one. He saved you the trouble of having to dig up for words.

"I miss her too."

The words startle you. You want to correct his obvious grammatical misplacement of gender, but you already know that he is no longer talking about your brother. His eyes are fixed firmly on the road. You can tell that he has struggled to avoid talking about her for as long as he could; about what happened today, seventeen years ago. This is a side of Papa that you so rarely see, you almost forget it exists. The side that shows a vulnerable man, a heart torn to shreds by the cruelty of loss.

"I think of her too. Sometimes."

False. You think about her all the time. You think about her in the shower every morning as the cold droplets hit your naked back. You think about her while walking in town, looking for her eyes in the idle faces of women seated outside the National Archives on Moi Avenue. You were thinking about her that evening at the dam with Rhosa.

You struggle to hold on to bits and pieces of her; to old photographs, to foggy images, to stories your brother used to tell you; of the woman whose absence has marked your life for the past seventeen years.

You park the car on the city council parking lot, just outside the Cooperative Bank building. As you alight, the cold city breeze brushes against your nose, carrying in it a whiff of smoke. In the smoke, you inhale the scent of memories, of yesterdays you would rather forget. Suddenly, you are in your family's old living room in Kondele, Kisumu, on an evening many, many nights ago.

*

There was a strangeness about the way Mother danced that Friday night. She was holding your hands as she waltzed on the living room carpet, her head swaying to the reeling tune of Princess Jully's "Dunia Mbaya" on the transistor radio. Papa was seated on the striped sofa, sipping diluted whiskey from a glass as your ten-year-old brother gobbled down what was left of the strawberry cake. It was the third day of April, 1998. Your sixth birthday. Your last, with her. Four months later, 7th August 1998, she would walk into her new job at Cooperative Bank head office in Nairobi. On that first day at work, there would be a terror attack, an explosion, and her soul would rise with the black fumes that engulfed a mourning city.

*

There are still days when you wake up wishing you were those black fumes, following your mother into nothingness. But you think of Rhosa and you smile. You are not black fumes.

You are here, at the memorial park, standing in front of the grey board with names of the victims of the attack. There are others here as well; each handling their sadness in their own way. In the dim glow of candlelight, you watch as a middle-aged man takes off his hat and lays a wreath, with a tremble in his left hand, as it clutches desperately to white rosary beads. He stands there for a few more seconds, then rushes out without looking back. A young woman holds her toddler son in her arms as she hums a tune, her pinky finger on one of the names engraved on the stone parchment: Salome Mandebele. Maybe the name belonged to her sister, maybe her mother, maybe the woman that was never her mother but raised her as her own child. She mumbles a few words and then holds on tighter to her son. The little boy just turns his head; eyes darting from one corner to the next, looking at the people gathered around him, staring into their furrowed faces that betray a longing for lost loves; himself oblivious, nonchalant.

Papa is moving his right hand over his left ring finger, stroking his wedding band. He takes a few steps forward, settles a few paces in front of you and you know it is because he does not want you to see his glistening eyes. You can feel the wetness on your own face and you are glad he moved away. You think of your brother. This is the first year you are doing this without him. You wonder what he is doing now. Maybe he does not even care. Maybe the pressures of a new life have made him forget.

It is 2am and you are back in the car, branching at the intersection off Haile Selassie Avenue and joining Uhuru Highway. The road is fairly empty, a sharp contrast to the motionless backlog of traffic that makes it hell on weekday mornings. You look at the man seated next to you and wish you knew him better than you do.

"Papa, do you still love her?"

The words just escaped before your lips could catch them. Like they had been floating just beneath your tongue. He turns his face to you, for a slight second, then turns to face the window on his passenger side. He remains mum, perhaps surprised at the question. He pulls down the window and lets the noisy, cold air blow into his face. You instantly regret asking the question. You want to apologise and ask him to forget it, but he lets out his voice with a slight tremor.

"Sometimes, I hate her for dying."

The silence that follows is no longer the laboured silence between two people who do not know what to say. It is the silence of a daughter who finally realises that her father has felt exactly as she has felt for the last seventeen years. It is the silence of a father who has laid himself bare to his daughter, and in doing that has found peace. A silence that says you finally understand each other, you feel each other's pain. It is the silence of a love that does not need words to express it.

This is it. The perfect opportunity has presented itself here. It had been nibbling on your thoughts ever since you stepped into the car, you just did not know how to say it. You do not know how people are supposed to start such conversations. But you have to say it. You can feel that it is now or never. It is time to tell him about Rhosa. It is time.

"I have met the love of my life."

It makes your insides wobble, the way he turns to look at you and a smile forms on his face. He need not say anything. That warm look, that silent smile, is paradise.

"And when do I meet this lucky man?"

"Girl."

"Pardon me?"

"She is a girl, Papa. And I am the lucky one."

A tense silence. The end comes in a forced, icy whisper.

"Oh."

Levels

Doreen Anyango

Jesus owes us a miracle. And he knows it too. My mother will not let him forget. I always know it is morning when I hear the gentle singsong reminder of her plight to the Lord. And then she is off to the market. I know it is night when I am awoken by her howls and shouts. At night, her remonstrations take on a more urgent and forceful tone. What doesn't change is the length or content of the prayers. A session is an hour long, beginning with a prayer in four parts: 1. She tells Jesus of her faith in him. 2. She tells him how much she has suffered. 3. She protests her innocence. 4. She demands to be remembered. She then goes over these parts in no particular order. Repeatedly, with more overlap, so that what started out as distinct coalesces into a wandering formless rant in tongues.

Today, there was no gentle morning reminder to Jesus. She was running late for church. She is there now, making her case closer to the source. The red plastic clock on the wall has been stuck at ten past five since I have been here, so I can't tell what time it is when I am startled by the sound, like someone throwing stones on the roof. It picks up pace and in no time I feel trapped in a metallic contraption pelted by billions of tiny stones. I had forgotten how loud the rain can be on an iron roof.

My mother has prepared for the rain for months. The bottom shelf of the large open-faced wall unit that covers one of the shorter sides of our small rectangle of living space is empty. The things that should be there — a green *kaveera* of charcoal, a charcoal stove, a heap of green bananas, a kerosene stove, a large bucket for dirty utensils, a small stool for sitting on while cooking — now find themselves squeezed in with the usual second-from-bottom shelf occupants: saucepans, plastic plates and cups, a flask, sugar, salt and spices.

This one room is all at once bedroom, kitchen, living room and store. The bed on which I spend my days and share at night with my mother takes up the other shorter side, directly opposite the open-faced wall unit. The two (only slightly) longer sides of the rectangle enclose our assortment of other household items strewn about: a high round table on which sits a small colour television and my mother's small rechargeable radio, six dining-set chairs without an accompanying table, basins, buckets and brooms stacked on a high stool. The curtain at the lone window is white with green flowers, and looks like it was cut to fit the dimensions of the window. The lone electric socket is high up on the wall above the TV table.

The air in this house is hard to breathe, even with fully functional lungs and the solitary window thrown open. The sound of raindrops on the roof seems to seep some of the limited air out of the sealed room. I feel like I am suffocating with each breath I take. I am tired of looking up at the iron-sheet roof with the black strings of cobwebs in the wooden support beams and the bare light bulb that my mother forgot to turn on so that the room is in a semi-dark, late-evening state.

It is no easy feat to roll over onto my side. The heaviness in my chest wobbles and sets off a sharp pain like a knife cutting upwards towards my throat. The view is no better on my side. I am face-to-face with the open-faced wall unit piled high with our stuff. The unit was a gift to my mother from the carpenter who had a workshop down the road many years ago. He probably gave it to her in the hope that a sturdy piece of furniture fashioned with his own hands would improve his credentials as a potential suitor. My mother graciously accepted his gift and let him pursue her. Behind his back she would scoff at his audacity — hmmn, a mere carpenter? *Mulalu?*

That poor carpenter is long gone, but his gift has served us well over the years. We know that the water never rises beyond the top of the bottom shelf. Emptied of its contents as it is now, the evidence of years of being submerged in water is clear: the inside of the bottom shelf is covered in white-and-green blotches and the plywood at the back is a greenish-black color. The walls of our rectangle of living space have also turned a dark green where they meet the floor and are covered in grey-green splotches and streaks all the way up to the roof. My mother's attempts at redecoration just make this evidence of decay all the more glaring. The floor is covered in a new plastic carpet with stripes of lime green and white. The door is also new and metallic and painted a dull green. There remains in the still air a faint whiff of paint mixed in with the usual musty tone of the house. The blanket is scratchy on my skin and I manage to push it off. I am thirsty and my tongue feels like something dead and furry in my mouth. But for a few moments at least, I can breathe easier on my side.

It is hard to pinpoint where exactly the water enters from. There is no stream gushing in through the small gap between the door and door frame. There is no tell-tale drip drip sound from holes in the roof. But suddenly there is water on the floor and with it comes a strange creeping kind of cold that is nothing like the winter cold I loved so much. I would walk in it for hours, the snow crunching under my feet. The cold blasts of air that made my face numb and my nose run also made me feel acutely alive. I guess cold and wetness are only pleasant when the promise of warm safe interiors is not far behind. Otherwise it just feels like this is all that makes up the universe — the clamour of raindrops on the roof, the invisibly rising water, and the strange creeping cold that starts from my covered feet and works its way up. I pull the scratchy blanket up to my chin and content myself with the view of the wall unit.

Shelf number three contains our good utensils for special occasions. They haven't been used since I have been back. This good stuff was brought down and dusted off during my childhood when the relatives from Kalungu came to visit. My mother would take the day off from the market and I would watch the glow on her face and hear the pride in her voice as she basked in their admiration. She was the one who had fled a bad marriage and made it across to the big city. She never let them forget it, often pausing mid-conversation to shake her head and without ever going into specifics, mention how hard it was making it in Kampala. And I believed that for a while – that my mother and I had made it.

Then I went to school and learnt other things along with my ABCs. Like the fact that there were levels. If your mother sold tomatoes in Kalerwe market and you lived in a one-roomed house in Bwaise, you were firmly in with the bottom crowd. You had not made it. But I learnt from my mother that that needn't necessarily translate into misery. Scratchy blankets and flooding houses could be comfortable. Happiness might even be found in them. Things could always be worse. And so when I had to drop out of high school in Form 3 because my mother couldn't afford the school fees, I understood that I would just have to do my best with the situation.

Shelf number four is for my mother's stuff. Taking pride of place is a framed photograph of my mother and me. We have on matching make-up: bright-red lipstick and thick arches of pencilled-on eyebrows. It was a celebratory portrait to commemorate the new bartending job I had landed in Muyenga, which is where Greg happened.

He would come in at eight every evening and sit at the same corner table where the light was decent. He always had a big brown book with him and only looked up from it to signal a waitress and growl for another Club beer. I wondered if he had many big brown books or if it was the same one he read with such singular concentration every evening. One day I gathered the courage to ask him. He looked up with a surprised "It speaks!" look on his face, as if all I was supposed to be was the automaton that delivered a chilled Club beer posthaste at the lifting of his hand. He told me there were several big brown books on philosophy. He was reading a whole series. Did I know what Philosophy was?

My mother met him once. We had her over for lunch a few

months after I moved into his apartment. Greg cooked. My mother showed up in a garish pink ensemble of punctured cloth. I had to translate back and forth between them. My mother asked what the mushy stuff on her plate was. Did he think she had no teeth? Why was there no meat? Greg kept smiling a tight condescending smile that made me want to slap him. I translated only the good stuff and embellished with some pleasantries of my own. I had expected at least some pretence of disapproval from my mother. Greg was old enough to be her father. When he went in for his nap after lunch and my mother and I sat at the balcony sipping mango juice and looking out at the lake, I was mentally working out how to convince her that the relationship was a good one. Only there were no protests from her. She poked me painfully in the ribs with her elbow and smiled a wide smile of approval. Greg and I got married soon after.

It was late on a winter afternoon when I first set foot on American soil. As the glass airport doors swished open of their own accord to let us out, the blast of cold air on my face was like an ice-fisted punch. I took an involuntary step back. Greg's grip on my hand tightened. "Careful," he said, "it's slippery; there's ice on the ground."

My mother is very proud of the fact that I lived in America. The tone of voice she uses when she slides that little fact into conversations — "You know, my daughter was in America for many years" — leaves the impression that I am more worldly than I actually am. The truth is, I never left Durham, North Carolina. I stayed home and cooked and cleaned for Greg and saved as many dollars as I could to send home to my mother. Greg also let me attend night school. Not because he cared about the improvement of my mind per se. He said I was too dependent on him and often seemed irritated by my presence in his living space. "Why do you have to be so here all the time?" he would look up from his newspaper with a frown and ask. Night school was a way to get rid of me for a few hours.

The topmost shelf of the wall unit has my stuff from America. Seven years of my life compressed into four small suitcases. I had left Uganda without any intention of ever coming back. The plan was that I would establish myself and send as much as I could to my mother. I was determined that I would put up with whatever I had to if I knew my mother was out of Bwaise. And I did put up with a lot. Leaving America was the furthest thing from my mind when the plan got messed up.

Greg died from a sudden heart attack. In his will, he left everything to a daughter I'd never met in the seven years we were married. She showed up for the funeral cloaked in black leather and gave me a week to leave her house. I had just enough for a one-way ticket back to Entebbe.

My mother was ecstatic when I showed up at her market stall in the airport taxi. I asked her for directions to where she now lived. She laughed. "*Kyokka* Linda, you mean you have forgotten your home?" I thought she was joking.

Later that evening as I sat on a dining-set chair missing a table, probably the same one I had been sitting on as an eight-year-old when she had told me about what goes where during sex, she explained matter-of-factly that she had only meant to increase our money. They had seemed like good Christian folk, the saving-group people. And the interest rates had been too good to be true. But I was not to worry, she said, God would surely remember us and exact vengeance on our behalf. For starters, I was back. It was a miracle! Hallelujah! She no doubt assumed that I had bundles of dollars stashed away in one of the suitcases.

It took me a while to think of a plan. I decided to look for Simon. He had hooked me up with the Muyenga job and in my desperation, he seemed like a logical starting point. The bar in Muyenga was still operational but under different management. The new manager was kind enough to tell me that Simon was now in the real estate business and direct me to his offices in an arcade in downtown Kampala. I got on a bodaboda back to town and my excitement mounted with each metre of road we covered. Real estate would be much better than bartending, more respectable. And I was no longer a high-school dropout: I had finished high school in America no less, and right before Greg died I had finished my studies for a degree in communication studies from the community college. I could definitely do real estate.

The reception was spacious and furnished with new Chinese furniture. *I could work here*, I thought as I waited. *It wouldn't be a bad start.* When, after almost an hour of waiting, I was ushered into Simon's equally spacious office, I had to remind him who I was. Not long before, when I had been in his office at the back of the bar asking for a job, he had offered me expensive alcohol and hadn't been able to keep his hands off me. Now he seemed in a hurry to get rid of me. He kept typing on his tablet, not really hearing how much I needed this opportunity.

To make it clear how far I was willing to go, I moved closer to him on the slippery faux leather couch and put my hand on his thigh. That got his attention, but not in the way that I had hoped. He looked like he might throw up and asked me to leave his office. I had left America because I convinced myself I didn't know how to fight in the American way. It was becoming clear that I didn't know how to fight in Uganda either.

That realisation seems to have triggered the rapid decline of my lungs. That, and the musty air in the house. And all those years of breathing in Greg's cigarette smoke. And that was only the second most revolting thing about him. The first? In all those years, I never got over the feel of his heaving loose-fleshed body on mine. And then, third onwards to almost infinity, I put up with insults and constant reminders that without him I would be nothing. I had to. Because I had a plan: put up with whatever I had to while milking as many dollars out of him to get my mother out of Bwaise. And all so he could die and leave everything to a daughter he hadn't seen in seven years. And all so my mother could lose all our money in some quack saving scheme. And now I am getting angry again.

It has been hours at least and the rain shows no signs of relenting. The water level in the house has risen and is almost at the top of the bottom shelf, which I now notice is the same height as the bed on which I lie. It wouldn't be such a bad thing if the water rose and rose and filled the little house and burst the door open and took me along with it. My mother has raised the charcoal to a higher shelf but forgot to raise me. I need a change of view as my neck is starting to feel a little sore.

I see it as I struggle back onto my back: big, black, beady-eyed and rushing towards me on the surface of the invisibly rising water. Before I have time to think, I scramble up into the corner of the bed. As my heart settles back into its normal rhythm, I become aware of the position I am in. I am sitting with my chin on my knees and my arms wrapped around my legs. Just a few seconds ago, I thought such a move would surely kill me. The big, black, beady-eyed thing is not big at all, just a regular-sized rat. I stare at it a long while as it floats on the water.

The rain is still pelting the roof when the door is pushed open and my mother wades in. She has a black *kaveera* on her head, muddy shoes in one hand and a five-litre jerrycan in the other. She looks around the house as if shocked by its state, although she stuffed all our bottom-shelf stuff onto the second shelf months ago in preparation for this exact scenario. She doesn't ask me how I am doing or why I am sitting up. She puts the shoes in the corner of her shelf and the five-litre jerrycan of holy water on the bed next to me.

"You have no idea how hard I had to fight to get that one," she says, and turns around so I can see the rip in her soaking-wet top. Without turning back to look at me she says, "The man of God said this is strictly for drinking." Still without turning to look at me, she picks up a bucket and starts to scoop water out of the house.

Like Eyes Liquid With Hope

Bura-Bari 'Vincent' Nwilo

Today, I am Oga, the alternate Oga of the house. It is a very good thing. I can go to the Big Oga's wardrobe and pick any of his big, nice-smelling clothes and wear. I may wobble in his coat, but that would only be until I start drinking beer. But some words sef has issues. 'Wobbling!' It is a bad word meant for small people like me who have very small flesh. People like Oga who talk too much grammar must have invented it to suppress persons like me who only finished primary school in the village and worked secondary on the farm with mama. My university is inside a big man's house as a cleaner and general messenger. It does not have anything to do with him and his size. Wobbling! It is me. The word has me as its profile picture. Which kain yeye thing is that? Anyway, I don't have to worry my head about the trouble that won't finish. English is madness. Who does not know it? Is it not the fear of English that drove the baboon into the forest? Won't it have been like me and you or so? If I fight this big word today, won't the people who own the world invent another bigger one?

People are heartless. They have taken their hearts into their palms and rubbed it with so much nonsense. Nothing in this world moves them. They could bring one that would break my jaw and make me totally useless. Will I keep fighting big big words until the world finishes? Who has that kind of power? Do I look like Jesus Christ that will go and carry the wahala of people on his head and follow them and go and die on a cross? Am I foolish? Was I born today?

Had Cecilia Deemua, my wonderful mother, given birth to a national mumu in Dukana? Hian. This thing is really causing me to fear oh. Hm. But as for my Oga, I can touch his shoes or even try it on. I can walk about and make the noise that won't pass through the big door or that nonsense gateman will run his stupid mouth and spoil my Egusi soup with his yeye Okra soup.

It is a good thing to be the alternate Oga. But Nneka won't respect me. That girl has problem with her head. Her kitchen-office has made her begin to think that she is equal with me in rank. She is too strong inside her head. If you talk one she will talk one hundred. Yes. One hundred words in one small minute. Who does that kind of thing? Her mouth runs like borehole. She would say: "See this yeye Ogoni boy oh. Na, you I come city come work for? You don't know that I am getting married soon to a rich man and I will be in my husband's house, commanding house-boys like you wey no get fear for eye? You hear?"

She is like that. She no get even small respect like this, small one that can fit inside tin-tomato container. I mean the small tin-tomato oh. She dey behave like say dem no use hot water press sense into her head when she was born. If I call her and say: "Nne, come! Bring me garri and soup with roasted meat," she fit even slap me sef. She go come and stand for my front, shake her yansh and tell me to go jump inside lagoon and die. You see, see women of these days? Dem no get fear of God inside their body. In short, God has died and been buried inside their heart.

If I were her I would treat me like an alternate Oga, whose situation can change tomorrow. Situation changes oh. I have seen a man who started as a boy in his Oga's house. Today, when he drives, his Oga will carry computer and look the type of car that his boy is now driving. He is proud of the boy. He goes to everywhere with high shoulder, preaching what a better Oga he was to Rufus. Yeye dey smell. But Nneka won't even treat me like the temporary Oga with potential. No. Sense no dey inside her dictionary. In fact, if you carry two hands open inside her dictionary, na either carrot, green pepper, yellow tomatoes, or vegetable na you go see. Nothing wey get value settle inside that her head. Imagine sey she humble herself, serve me food, won't I sit and enjoy mysef and add two minutes fat to my bones? If she did I would have myself all the food in the house and chop until I am tired. I would sit and she would bring me water to wash my hands, kneeling down of course. But whether she likes it or not, I am the alternate Oga and with or without food, no one will spoil my groove.

I will not allow that arrant nonsense in this house. Na rat get house when Oga comot. Today na my own Christmas and anybody wey come become witch I will use prayer and fasting kill am. Oga told Madam that when Small Madam will come back that he will use Holy Water wey him bishop give am take bath Small Madam. But that one brought laughter. Madam laugh sotey she almost fall for ground. I did not know that there was so much laughter inside Madam all these years. Madam laugh Oga until shame come rub Oga face like powder. I go thief that Oga Holy Water take fight any witch wey come disturb me.

I will put on the TV and relax like my Oga and Madam. Oga and Madam would bring their heads to each other and shake it like they were small children. They would make their lips touch and then they would lick it. There is no madam here with me. Nneka is foolish. I cannot call her. But I can still imagine a madam being here oh. Wait oh, it does not have to be my own madam. The picture of my madam must not come into my head in Jesus name or I will die. My Oga can see it when he looks at me. I don't want trouble. I want to remain with Oga until he finally sends me to a technical college or even a university. Like Oga's children, I would be a big man. I would not be hungry. When I want anything, I will just deep hands into my pocket and buy a large loaf of bread and chop. I can also buy my own sardine, tease Nneka with it and make sure even a drop of oil from the can passes her by.

To be a big man is a very excellent thing. Big men put big offering in church and God blesses them with another bigger money. They walk about like big men, legs apart and hands in the air. Small road does not do them. They have big stomach too. They chop a lot. They talk big big things. They talk about big house and big problems. They marry very pretty women. Chei! I want to be a big man oh. I want to drive a big car, like Toyota Prado, like Oga. I want to stand up and talk and allow people who are not successful to sit down and talk about their poverty in silence. I want to be that big with big mouth.

Oga and Madam have gone to the airport to carry Small Madam. That pikin has been overseas since Madam gave birth to her. I hear she is eighteen and she has decided to come and see Madam and Oga in this country. But my Oga did not agree when the news began oh. Oga was afraid. Afraid was catching my Oga because he had gone to pick a form in his party. He wants to be a senator. He wants to go to Abuja and become a bigger man. In Abuja, he would be closer to the President and maybe he would buy a plane then. He can't park a plane in the garage so I don't know why he would buy it sha. But my Oga does not like stress. He wants everything to happen fast fast. He does not like to stand on the line when he goes to the airport. He does not like to stand on the line in the bank. When I follow him to the bank, he would sit down and I would stand on the line until they call his name: Chief Matthias Needam! He would write his signature and he would give me the bundle of money to carry to the car.

My Oga is a fine man. I like his fineness. He does not leave the house without looking at the mirror and talking fine things to himself: "I am the people's choice. Congratulations, Distinguished Senator Needam. You fought a magnificent battle."

My Oga does not like anything that makes his heart fly. If you have bad news, you go to Madam and tell her. Madam would be the one to pass the message to Oga in a way that it will sweet him and not make him become sick. If Oga wants you to buy him anything and you lose your money or chop it, as the case may be, you dare not talk to him. Bad news does not cross his gate. Big men are like that. I want to be a big man like there is no tomorrow.

Small Madam stays in America abi na London. But all is the same.

They have the same white people everywhere. I hear America is very very fine like paradise. Ah, paradise is sweet oh. When Jehovah Witness people bring their book and come show us the picture of paradise, you would want to stop bad things and wait for paradise. Animals plenty everywhere in paradise. Dem no dey even chop human being, lion and small pikin dey play inside garden. Chei. No upstairs, no motor, people just go to anywhere on foot and they have smiles on their faces. What I don't like about it is that water easily carry people's houses and kill them in oyinbo land and that may be the same in paradise.

In the village, we had a big river but a river never left its house to another man's house to carry him and kill him and destroy his house. The rivers have respect for the people and all they do. I think that is because the people respected the river well well. They gave it eggs and hot drinks. They go and talk to the river and apologise to it when they shit inside the water or when they mistakenly go there when their monthly visitor is around. In the village, though no light, life is very sweet. In the night we will sit around, chopping strong corn and be telling stories of tortoise and how smart it is. In the village you do not stay on the line for water. You do not wait for anybody. If your body is hot you just jump into the river and wash up. But here, hmm, it is not like that.

My Oga likes his daughter. When Small Madam said she would jump into a plane and come to Nigeria, Oga nearly died. He does not like talks like that. He shouted and quarrelled with Madam that it is the stubborn head of Madam that Small Madam has carried. He said that if Small Madam come into Nigeria all those small small boys will come and be knocking on the door every day. He said that those mumu who are envious of him and his new desire will go and arrange with jobless graduates and go and kidnap her precious daughter.

There is nothing he did not say to Big Madam but nothing worked. The more he talked, the more the calls came into the telephone. Person can hear Small Madam shouting and screaming like say America is biting her skin comot. But small children can be very funny ehn. If I go to America today, tell me, what is that nonsense that will make me to come home? I will beg the oyinbo people to forget about my name and give me their own name. I will tell dem to forget Mene Deemua. I don't want to be called Mene again. They should call me Tomatoes or Fish. Oyinbo people have very funny names. They can call me Sardine sef. I will not mind. I will go to a place that is very fine and snap better photo and send it to the people who are here in Nigeria. When they look they will jump and appreciate Bari and tell themselves that they must leave Nigeria too. But my Oga will not send me to oyinbo land. He will make sure I wash the cars, follow him to the bank and iron his big big clothes. He would not bother me today. Hei. See Mene oh. Mene should enter inside a plane too and see how the other world looks like. In short, if Oga makes that mistake, I will go to America and disappear. I will not be seen again until I have become a very big man then I will buy a bottle of Schnapps aromatic drink and go to tell him that though I am a bad person for running away, my mind has been paining me for all the bad things I have done against him.

Maybe he will ask me to sit down. I will sit on the leather chair in the parlour, like a fellow big man and drink whiskey with him and laugh. He will talk politics with me and tell me he likes me. He will tell me that though I ran away, he is not so angry with me, that I am still his best friend. Ha. Me? Small Mene, a best friend of a big Oga like Chief Matthias Needam? Money can make a small man the best friend of a big man oh. Once you can speak very big English and pay for your own drinks and your own cigarette you will be loved by every big man. No big man wants to buy free drinks for anybody. In short, when a big man knows that you will not pay for your own drinks, he will tell you that something has happened and that he will not come to the meeting. That is if you are a big man small oh. But some of them will not even pick your call. They will watch your call and then sigh and chew kola nut.

Small Madam is really fine in the photo that Madam put on the wall. She looks like a mermaid, like a Mami Wata wey never sabi bad things. Madam is always proud of the picture. In the morning she will come and look at it and clean dust from it and laugh and be proud of herself. I like that. When I grow up too and have money as a big man and marry a wife I will have a daughter that will be as fine as Small Madam and I will train her abroad. I will send her to Imperial College, yes that is the place where Oga said he took Small Madam to. I will hang my daughter's photo in the parlour too and tell my friends about her school fees and how big it is. I will finish training her and when she wants to get married I will make sure she marry another big man.

Yes na. Big men do not marry small men. When a big man get pikin he will train him so that the poor man will not have the mind to approach her and say anything to her. In short, the only place they can meet is the church. But a big man can decide to use police inside the church and God no go vex. God does not vex for big men. They build the house of God. They can hire policemen to stand in church and watch the eyes of the people who will look in the direction of the daughter. I will be like that. I will have twenty policemen. I will make two walk with my daughter every day. Ten will work with me. Three will be at home. Five will be with my wife. All that will happen in our house will smell of police. Mosquito will be very afraid to even fly in my house. I will not hire somebody like yeye Johnbull, who will sleep and forget that he is a gateman. When Oga comes he would be shouting so much and the mumu will not even wake up. I would be the one to run from the house and open his gate for him and at the end of the month he will be the first to stop Oga when he wants to enter motor and ask for his salary.

But me, I like Johnbull. He has heart. He can meet anyone and ask for anything. I am very afraid and shy. I cannot even meet Lemene and ask for her hands for friendship. In the streets people who are small, people who I am taller than have girlfriends and I do not have. I do not have, not because I do not bother oh. It is because I do not have heart, the heart to tell a girl that this is what I feel inside my heart and that it is very unique.

Lemene is a fine girl. She is Chief Ikoma's daughter. Chief Ikoma's is not a proper chief oh. He calls himself chief. And everybody calls him chief also. He has a big cloth with lion head that he wears. I do not like him. It is Lemene that I love. When you see Lemene's smooth legs, you will shout for Jesus to come down and forget about heaven and his father's kingdom. Lemene is so beautiful that when people come to buy garri from them they drop change and never collect it back. They stammer and become like mumu. I love Lemene. I am not a mumu for her oh, but if she ask me to be a mumu, I will go inside the house, bath and rub very fine cream with fine aroma and become her mumu.

It is almost night. Oga has not come back. Madam has not come back too. I don't want trouble. I will love to go to Oga's room and try to wear his clothes or that fine shoe that shines like mirror. But the feeling may just sweet me so much and I will sleep off. And Oga will return and stand over me and say: "Look at him. Nincompoop! Do I pay Mene to be a goat? Do I keep him in my mansion so that when I am not around he will be a rat, run into my clothes without respect?" No. I don't want that. I want peace. I want to sleep in the parlour, on this leather chair and enjoy the cool breeze from the AC. They will wake me when they come. Oga will shout and I will jump up. If I do not, Nneka can be the new Mene for today. As for me, let me be the alternate Oga small.

Subtle Defence

Frances Ogamba

When I kneel on the hassock and try to whisper prayers to the variegated decorations of the pulpit, the altar where God supposedly lives or visits, I feel people's eyes staring, wondering why I worry, or why I even come here at all.

Sometimes I wonder how God sits in our church. Does he cross his legs on some invisible throne and smirk at our unreasonable requests? Does he mock us for having no knowledge of the formula for effective prayer? Or does he just sit there judging, deciding who lives or dies, who gets married to a lawyer and who doesn't? What could I possibly ask for? Do I say, "Lord, take this cross away from me," like Mama Dumdum sings every morning when she walks by my window? Do I have a cross? I have what many women think they need: a barrister husband, an excellent lawyer, so calm and handsome, courteous, soft-spoken, who doesn't allow me near market stalls, who doesn't let me know what prices inflated, and what a cup of egusi would cost if I bought the ground one. I have two little sons too. I get admiring stares when I trek to church with them in our matching outfits.

"She dey enjoy o," people always whisper.

Before Chuka the lawyer married me six years ago, my breasts stood like anthills in the middle of a farm. They were full and firm like a lump of foo foo in your right palm. I was barely out of high school and we had just moved to Onitsha from the village. I was buying ehuru for my mother's pepper soup at a stall by the road when

I noticed his eyes feeding on me. He parked his car in a nearby school field. I remember his car looking futuristic like in sci-fi movies. The glistening reflection of the sun's rays made it more impressive. He signalled me with a hand gesture and I couldn't resist going, just to take a closer look. He spoke good English and his voice thrummed on the edges of his words. When he smiled, the dimples on his cheeks sunk in as though poked by an object. He mentioned flowers and compared me to them. He said I was ripe for plucking, and his words made my cheeks quiver with shyness.

I dreamt of becoming a nurse or a caregiver. Though father died shortly after I finished high school, my ambition didn't grow faint with his memories or shrivel with the wreath on his grave. It came alive every new year, especially when the brightness of Lawyer's car entered my eyes.

Mother kept rubbing her palms together to keep her excitement down. Her eyes were the rays of a rising sun.

"Lawyer will send you to the university and send some money to us. When you become a nurse, you will fund your brothers' businesses. Ensure you don't annoy him," Mother continued singing in my ears until he married me three months later and took me to Port Harcourt. Pitakwa: the oil city.

At first, he didn't let me do anything. He cooked all our meals because mine didn't meet his standard. He didn't let me near market stalls or to walk the streets except in his company. I could go out only when we were together, and when he wanted to go alone, he locked me in.

"Baby, you don't know — some women come here and leave their husbands for other men..."

"Tufia. That one na abomination," I interjected hoping to convince him that I was different.

He cupped my face in his sturdy palms and told me how beautiful I was and how much he was scared to lose me. He bought me dresses that were twice my size because he said he didn't want other men gobbling me up with their eyes.

Two weeks after I arrived in Port Harcourt, he left the doors unlocked in his haste, and drove out. I ran out of the house with no particular destination in mind. It was the first time I really saw the houses that shone like they were dipped in yellow and pink and white paints because all along I saw them in my husband's eyes, the way he wanted me to see them. The zinc sheets were all black like the ehuru in my mother's pepper soup. The women here, just like the Onitsha women, wore red lips and had full heads of hair. I roamed the nearby streets and took lungfuls of the hot afternoon air. I also dared to walk close to the main road to see what type of cars sped past, what words bus conductors used, what words the sign posts showed...

I stood there motionless as punches rained on me. Everything blurred and my cheeks felt as though they had been torched. I saw stars as I clutched my abdomen. I went into the toilet a couple of hours later in such excruciating pain to ease myself. I felt a pull from within, as though something was having fun at pushing me back and forth. My thigh muscles, like wet clothes being prepped for spreading, squeezed and stretched repeatedly until something left my body. I don't remember crying or screaming, but I remember pulling the toilet handle and flushing down something I never knew was there. My mother says it isn't right to mourn something you didn't know you had. So I let that baby go and I emerged from the toilet like I had just finished easing myself of some waste product. The two baby boys I had later were the fighters that survived direct punches to the midriff, constant cussing that generated high blood pressure, falls on the ceramic toilet sink, and preeclampsia.

Today, Lawyer is nowhere to be found and has left the door open. The cold breeze sharply contrasts with the hot sun. The silence is becoming loud enough to make me want to run outside and fill my eardrums with sounds: horn blares maybe, or happy school children playing on their way home. I love to feel the Port Harcourt soil on my toes too, especially these untarred roads where sand grains lie longing for a kick. I walk down the road kicking the sand viciously before I take a detour and head into the church. The pulpit still has its decorations, though new styles – as though God has changed his style of reclining on the throne. I kneel and hope for a divine presence or the supernatural peace associated with sacred places to possess me. I walk back home after a futile wait. Lawyer is home with the boys. I see certain trepidation in my sons' eyes, but I try to feel nothing.

"I went to church," I say before he asks.

He doesn't reply.

"Daddy says we shouldn't talk to you," my first son tells me in confidence as I tuck him into bed. "You can talk to me sha," he says sleepily.

I smile at the manner "sha" plays out on his lips. I sing them lullabies, stitching together my voice like a worn-out gown so it doesn't tear into sobs. My lines coax them into the dream realm.

"I am going out," Lawyer mutters and bangs the door behind him. He doesn't say where.

I am a peaceful woman, so I don't block the doorway shaking my fingers in my man's face — threatening to cut off his boner or grizzling about his inattention. I let him go like Jesus would; I set him free to the world without surmises of how he may be gawping at erect breasts and full buttocks. I let him in at midnight, just like every other night when he brushes past me looking sated. His snores are like sounds of pump water tickling my eardrum until I can no longer bear it. So I tap him lightly, unlike other nights. Suddenly, his right hand begins groping for the wrapper knot at my waist. I move the inquisitive hand away gently.

"Chu, you dey snore. I no fit sleep," I whisper, not very sure if I should have said that.

His hand is reaching for me again. I want to chop it off with my teeth. I hit it instead and, in response, he slaps my cheeks three times in quick succession.

"Why are you slapping me? Wetin I do you? Oh, I cannot

complain about your snores again?" I demand as the pain comes from somewhere around my lungs and settles in my throat as a scream.

"You have no right to remove my hand when I am reaching for what's mine."

"You never tire, Chuka? Aren't you just returning from her place? Her scent full your shirt sef."

"Shut up! Are you mad? How dare you raise your voice at me?" he growls and all the animosity I am familiar with prances around on his face from his nostrils to the holes in his irises.

"Chuka, you dey find trouble o. You dey –"

We are struggling now. He rips off my clothes like a maniac as I clutch on to nothing but my sagged breasts. He slaps me some more until I hear my son's cry in the next room. I stop fighting him. What is wrong with me? Does a woman deny her husband his needs?

My mother repeats the question days later when I sprawl on her corridor staring into space. She is picking egusi. I am playing with the shells.

"What is wrong with you? Does a woman deny her husband his needs?" she asks, and adds that a woman has no right to disturb her husband's sleep even if he vomits on her newly made hair. She says snoring is a sign that he is healthy. She says a whole lot of other things I decide not to remember.

I understand Mother's fears because my brothers owe their flourishing businesses to Lawyer's pocket. Mother's pepper soup joint also benefits from Lawyer's benevolence. She doesn't want to lose any of that and moreover she dreads being that woman whose daughter couldn't keep a man.

Lawyer returns home looking repentant. As usual, his promises fill up the living room and spill through the roof racks that our couches lose their balance and begin to swim in them.

"I will meet Pastor Emma for counselling. I promise you, we will go back to normal."

Normal? But there is no normalcy with us. He goes down on his knees like he always does. I don't believe the emotion displayed on his face, so ugly that it pleats into many folds. I don't believe the tears gathering beneath his lashes like an impending storm. But I'm tired of the war, and a little peace would do. He leans in to kiss me, his short arms struggling to go round me. I try to return his embrace, but something strong restrains my hands from leaving my sides. He doesn't complain but he keeps ogling me. We make a baby that night; after the scan I name her Brianna. I am actually excited for this one because she is going to be someone to share my powder and lipstick with. Lawyer is excited too. He touches my cheeks when he is in a good mood, other times he just rants about insignificant things. He doesn't hit me. He still locks me up.

I feel an uncontrollable desire to nibble apples. I want to protest, you know, like the Aba women riot of 1929 in British Nigeria. I fetch a hammer from the basket that contains his car tools and let out my frustration on the keyhole until the irons hang loose like a dead dog's dentition. I dare Lawyer to hit me for breaking out of the house. I dare Chuka to lay a finger on the mother of his so-badly-wanted baby girl.

"I am the man. You are nothing. Idiot!" His seething rage slices his voice into a husk, into a strong thick husk that takes a man's form and hits me with this portable water heater I had plugged in for his evening bath. He whacks me across the bridge of my nose and I stagger backwards and touch the sore point. Blood stains my fingernails. My sons would want to know about the brown scars spanning across my face like blight stains on mangoes and I will tell them that I had a bad fall — the type that affects only the face. My little son is crying, but Lawyer doesn't let me go carry him. He keeps threatening the boy with a sound beating if he doesn't shut up. He slaps me when I remind him that the boy is only a child. Then the boy gets tired at some point and sleeps off without dinner. His brother joins him later.

There is a loud knock on the door. I wash my face quickly and open it to find a small crowd of neighbours standing on the porch.

"Shebi no wahala, Sista? We hear shouting before so we say make we come check," says their spokesman, the elderly driver who lives five doors away, waving his torch in every direction. The crowd nods their approval, a sign that he speaks their minds.

I smile while telling them that my little boy has rashes and they irritate him and make him cry. They proffer apologies and my smiles show them the way out. You see, a woman should always be graceful.

Sometimes, I want to tell Lawyer about school. I want to remind him of his six-year-old promise, but I cannot find my voice in my throat. It seems I have lost it like I did my taste buds. I tower over him, all five feet seven, and eighty-four kilograms of me yet I am small — around him, in his bed, and in his life. I am nothing.

Sunday. Our pastor is preaching directly to my soul. He says that prayers work with actions; and that people should physically uproot what has emasculated them spiritually, whatever renders them pallid. When life launches heavy blows at our midriff, what do we do? How do we evade the punches meant for us but thrown at our unborn babies instead? What do we do when we get raped even with the ring shining on our fourth finger? How do we duck the constant jabs at our emotions? As the pastor's strong voice lends force to the admonishment, I flow along with him like a rivulet; I swim along shores until the church choir takes me up from where the pastor stopped. They sing Boseyiye and I loosen myself up to the beat. I can feel Lawyer's stare on my back but I care less — for now. My younger son is laughing at me and trying to dance too. The older one is shy and is tugging at my skirt to stop. The entire congregation seems to be swaying to the tunes because of me. I take myself back in time to my mother's pepper soup joint, my two brothers, the customers, the dances, Mama's laughter, Mama's chidings...

I dance galala. I dance skelewu. I dance shoki.

"Na church we dey o and you don marry sef," I hear the catechist's wife whisper behind me.

I give her a long look; shake my head as her reminder sets me adrift the pathway of more excitement. I dance shakiti bobo. I try to crush my pain by moving my feet. Does she know battering, miscarriages, or house imprisonment? Do her ribs break under the weight of her man's shoes? The congregation is clapping alongside the bass drum and a small crowd is gathering around our pew. The pride in my sons' eyes outshines the glimmer of anger on Lawyer's face as he tries unsuccessfully to mask his irritation. The frenzied atmosphere returns to a serene one when the song ends. A handful of people shake my hands after the service, and others pass me congratulatory waves from afar. I am something here. I actually exist. I bask in the waves of excitement until a slap from the palms I know so well burns my cheek in our living room, punishing me for all the dance styles I advertised in the house of God.

I am making jollof rice for the children, and the little salt remaining in the house will not sharpen the taste enough. Lawyer is out so I turn all his trouser pockets inside out, rummaging and hoping to find even a torn ten-naira note. A fifty-naira note thankfully falls out instead, accompanied by something else. I bend with difficulty and scoop something up — ash liquid tied in a sagging rubber sachet. I know that Lawyer cheats on me, but this first evidence hits me like bad air. I arrange the mess I created and run to Mama Dumdum's shop to buy salt. I want to leave after buying the salt, but the weight of the ongoing gossip glues my feet to the shop pavement. I am not the only mesmerised audience. Other women are standing there listening as the black nylons in their hands swing impatiently like Lawyer's mood. The speaker is talking with a charisma that can only be associated with experience. She is talking about ute, a spiritual mat that can be used to make an enemy somnolent or even fully asleep all through life. She boasts of the number of people she has sent to this temporary spiritual slumber. She is reading out her phone number for people to contact her. Some of the women are bold enough to scribble it on scraps of paper they borrow from Mama Dumdum's debtor's book. I cram the eleven numbers instead and briskly walk away.

What am I doing? Why am I doing this? I'm not sure, but I am transferring the number from my head to my telephone, one of the few things Lawyer bought that surprised as well as shocked me. He always ransacks my phone like a wardrobe though, so I save the number as Nwanyi Dustbin. I eat the rice when it is cooked, but it tastes like something else — like a potion that may come with ute. It is a Saturday, so I rest well. I don't let Lawyer's tantrums get to me. They don't stop my galala dance in church on Sunday. I dial the number later when the image of the used condom I found in Lawyer's pocket flashes in my mind. But Lawyer stays home on Monday and Tuesday. The eager voice of the woman is always disappointed each time I call to give excuses.

One afternoon Lawyer is asleep, so I sneak to the Ada-George Road to meet her. There are no shrines, or red banners or oaths like I feared. Just a discreet ash powder tied in a nylon sachet accompanied by somewhat complicated instructions:

No contact with water.

Do not cough around it.

To be kept in a cool place and out of prying eyes.

I secure it with a knot at one end of my wrapper and run home, pausing at intervals to ensure it is intact. I barely concentrate on events. I have replied my son's questions twice with "Ute." He must be wondering what that means. I decide to make ofe Owerri for Lawyer. It is his town's delicacy and he will be excited to eat it. He hasn't eaten any of my meals in a while. I watch as the powder melts and becomes all the ingredients I need for spicing up the meat. I see gladness flickering in his eyes as he devours the soup, munching on the many fish and meat pieces.

"Thank you, Ma," he says, patting my arm, and his skin feels soft; softer than the foo foo wraps lying in his plate. I imagine his eyes, like a dying torch, twinkling dimly until the entire room becomes pitch-black.

I borrowed some money from Mama Dumdum to make that soup a reality.

I have rented a new shop at Farm Road where I sell clothes. I have access to the market where I can go hussle commodity prices with other women and get a chance to complain about the rain, the hot sun or the fact that I'm not home and rain may drench my laundry. Baby number three will be due soon, and my mother will come for omugwo for the first time. My new wardrobe chokes with ankara pieces, buba, lesi and joji. I attend driving lessons on Saturdays, too.

"You will go to school for a part-time programme," Lawyer tells me one evening.

I give a testimony in church about how a seven-year-old marriage has suddenly become more interesting than a honeymoon.

The brethren echo "Amen!"

Then they start singing, "God of miracle, na my papa ooh!"

I still dance galala, skelewu and shoki.

The Dreamers Will Be Safe

Sese Yane

The clock read a few minutes to midnight. My eyes followed the girl as she walked across the diner. She talked to the man in a tweed jacket and made as if she might untie her pinafore, before putting her hands in her pocket. Isn't it strange... I was thinking to myself, but then could not complete the thought because the girl was now walking towards me, or perhaps towards the kitchen... indeed towards the kitchen.

I shouted after her, "Maggie, how about... I mean, that bumper... does it still... you know?" She hesitated before continuing towards the kitchen, and I shouted, "Maggie, did you see that story about the goat on TV, funny eh?" and that got to her and she gasped, "God, poor goat!" and we both laughed before she disappeared into the kitchen. The sound of china clanked behind me.

I observed the man. He appeared scrawny and awkward as he rose from his seat, which in turn made a brief screeching sound. He bent to pick up something, and then rose with a briefcase. I watched him walk towards me. He stood before me, bent again, rose. His face twitched, and then he handed me a note he had fumbled out of all the pockets on his clothing.

"How much is your change?"

"I believe it's... two-fifty?"

I pulled the register, dropped his note there, lifted two-fifty and handed it over to him. I don't remember seeing him leave, but when

I thought about him again I noticed he wasn't there, as if I had misplaced him.

And now I found myself wondering about the darkness outside the diner. I thought of the man. I imagined him lost somewhere in the darkness outside, swallowed by it, or floating... Perhaps wading is the correct action, I thought, wading until he found himself inside a house... a familiar house (but don't all houses look ghostly anyway?) and people he recognised emerged one after the other like light bulbs coming on until a maximum that his truth could allow, oh God, thank God our traveller was safe.

The three of them walked out of the kitchen; the girl was now zipping up her white jumper, the other girl tying her hair behind her head, and the fat man was laughing.

"You'll close up, right?" said the fat man as he leapt behind the two girls like a toad, adjusting the red scarf around his neck.

"Sure," I shouted after them.

Once they were out of sight I would close up and walk to the venue, but until then I would stare at the door until I was sure it was time.

I thought of the silence in the diner and noticed that the silence was more of the absence of bodies than the absence of sound. And then I thought perhaps the silence was more of the presence of empty chairs than the absence of bodies, and that if there were no chairs then the absence of the bodies would not be felt. And then I thought maybe the silence was because of the lights. I heard the door open and when I looked up I saw a woman.

"We're closed," I heard myself say to her.

"Oh, God no," she said. "I just want a coffee, please."

The woman, who appeared to be in her mid-thirties, wore a green turtleneck sweater and a cream skirt. I pointed her to the booth and disappeared into the kitchen. When I came out, her black handbag was resting on the table on its side like an exhausted cat. She wore thick glasses. She did not have a scarf over her head, no. She did not have a face one could call stunning either, no. But it was a face one might call interesting.

"Thank you, thank you," she said when I placed the cup of coffee on her table.

I had never served anyone in the diner before and so I didn't know how to take my leave. But standing there over her I also noticed that I ought to have carried the cup on a tray and not by its handle.

Perhaps out of my awkward presence standing there next to her, she decided to ask me about the book I was holding. What it was about.

Taking the seat opposite hers, I said I didn't know. It didn't have a cover, as she could clearly see. It could be by a writer called Italo Calvino. Or perhaps it's by one called Julio Cortazar. Either way, it didn't matter really.

"You see, I don't know who these writers are."

But when someone had asked me in the past, "What are you reading?" I had sometimes said I was reading a book by Italo Calvino, and other times I had told them I was reading a book by Julio Cortazar. Depending. And even briefly I told some of them I was reading a book by Jorge Luis Borges, I said to her.

"I don't recall how this book came into my possession, you see."

I hadn't noticed that I had it until someone had asked me what book it was that I was reading. And I went on telling whoever cared to ask me where I had found it that I had torn it from a cat's paw at a dumpster.

"I have been saying it for so long that I now believe it to be indeed true. Though it's also quite possible that I accidentally walked it out of a library. You see, I used to work as a guard at the National Library."

There was a regular at the diner, however; a teacher, or so he claimed to be. He was always in a yellow suit and a yellow pocket-square and a yellow hat and carried along a walking stick. He was the one who told me that this book was by a writer called Italo Calvino. And then the following week he said it was not by Italo Calvino but indeed by someone else; a writer known as Julio Cortazar. And then the week after that he said it was not by Julio Cortazar but actually by Jorge Luis Borges. That's how it was with him. Every week he mentioned a new name. I even started looking forward to the new author of this book, the forthcoming authors, so to speak. And then one day he said he wanted nothing to do with literature and had taken interest in painting instead. He was studying Vermeer now. He'd already completed studying Goya, he told me.

"Painters are more interesting than writers," he said.

But musicians are the worst. Even though music is in fact closer to truth than painting and writing are. Music, he said, allows the listener to participate in creation, unlike writing and painting, which are exhibitionistic in nature. When we observe a painting or read a book we can only marvel at the genius of the creator. The creator never releases his work: he ties a leash around it and then dangles his creation on our faces, insulting us; he wants us to worship him; wants us to praise him for writing a "marvellous" novel or for a "spectacular" painting, I said to the girl.

Of course it was okay for her to smoke, I said, and she leant forward so that I could strike the match against the cigarette that was now dangling from her mouth.

I explained to her that we are moved by a particular painting because it is by Vermeer not because of its own attributes; therefore, we are moved by a Vermeer, which is to say that we are moved by Vermeer and not his painting. And a certain painting can fail to move us because we believe it is a forgery of a Vermeer. And then this same painting can move us again if we find that it is indeed by Vermeer, which is to say if we find out again that it is not by Vermeer it will stop moving us once again.

"I have never heard of Vermeer. Or Goya. But I have heard of Picasso," she said.

That's what the teacher says, of course. We like a story because it is by Kafka, not because of its own attributes; we are moved by Kafka and not by anything he writes, which is to say, his works are meaningless to us, until they are by him.

"I have heard of Kafka," she said.

But we sing along to a song we like. We participate. We cannot enjoy a song otherwise. And until the recent musician, this musician created by consumerism and capitalism, a song did not have a creator. And poetry did not have a writer either. It was simply there. The composer never came forward to claim the song. The poet did not come forward to claim the poem, until the novel. A novel can never exist without its writer, but a poem can. A painting can never exist without the painter either, because his name verifies the painting. But even with this new musician, who tries to claim the song as his own, just like the painter and the writer have been doing for quite some time now, we still manage to eliminate him when dealing with the song.

Only the uncultured know how to read a novel. Only an uncultured person like me could carry a novel around without bothering to acquaint himself with its writer, the teacher had said to me. He could never imagine doing such a thing. He was too sophisticated to just go about reading any other novel when he had "a painful backlog" of authentic writers to read. He had not finished reading everything by Proust, Dostoyevsky, Lispector, Gombrowicz, Walser, Bernhard, Sebald, Krasznahorkai, Mann, Musil, Handke, Murnane, Machado de Assis, not to mention the philosophers, the poets, the dramatists, the essayists, et cetera.

"He mentions their names over and over again to me, you see."

"I have heard of Proust," she said, shaking the ash off the cigarette to the floor.

But of course now he said he wanted nothing to do with literature any more. Because the books he was yet to read were greater in number than the years nature would allow him to exist and, even worse, writers worth reading were being born every year. Why should he read anything else if he had not read *The Demons*, for instance? Why should he be excited about our new writers when he could not even muster the emotional and intellectual temperament required to finish even one page of *The Passion According to G.H.*? But above all, literature was impure. A book made the writer, and the writer hardly told a story. He could never own a book like he could own a song. He could sing a song, but could never rewrite a book like Pierre Menard. And even Pierre Menard could only rewrite a book because he did not exist. As she could imagine, I too had no idea what the teacher meant by this, but it is something he said over and over in the diner.

I, on the other hand, had never read the book I was carrying. I only walked around with it and had been walking with it for almost a year now. So, as she could imagine, I didn't know what it was about.

"I have never found the need to read this book other than to carry it, you see."

But if she would come the following day to the diner, then I promised to tell her what the book was about after finding out from the teacher, who was sure to show up, and who had read the book at least five times, each time saying that it was better than the last time.

I sighed and sank in my seat, looking at her. The fluorescent tube above us was now two tiny light sabres on her glasses. Outside the diner, I could hear an occasional vehicle's motor buzzing by. All the while I had been speaking to the woman in the diner, I had been following the three of them (the two girls and the fat man) with my mind's eye into the night, and now I could see them at the other side of town nearing the apartment. I had not wanted to walk with them. I wanted to walk alone. I did not want them to see me taking the alleyway behind Main Street. And because I wanted only to close the diner after I was sure that there was no danger of catching up with them, I had decided to talk to the woman. But now, looking at her, and how she had placed her elbows on the table, clearly exhibiting signs of someone who was not ready to release me, slightly tilting her head in the manner women do in the diner when they are in the company of a cordial gentleman, I knew I had overplayed my hand. Out of my own naïveté and clear lack of tact, I had made a friend.

Her smile when she had asked me earlier whether she could get a coffee had reminded me of a certain girl I used to know. That's the only reason I had agreed to break protocol and allow her into the diner way past the official closing time.

"I felt as if I was being given an opportunity to right a wrong, you see."

Before I found work at the diner, I had worked at the National Library as a guard, and before that I had worked at the Municipal Hospital's cafeteria. One day, at the Municipal Hospital, a colleague had said to three of us that he had found himself a girl, but the girl was also owner of a "vindictive" cat that never left her side and scratched anyone who came close to her. He now wanted us to break into the house that night posing as robbers, shake him and his girl a little, take a few household items, but remember to take the cat with us as well. Of course we agreed to this.

"You don't know how difficult it is to find ski masks in this town."

If she would care to put herself in the shoes of a robber, then she would understand that being a robber is hard work. Of course, she should know that the world operates under the fallacy that robbers are simply lazy people who want to get things easily and for free, but that is far from the truth; it is much easier to work in an office where one's labour is pensionable and you get to work under sufficient lighting without the inherent dangers of a life of crime. The average robber has to exert himself more than a civil servant. A robber, as she could imagine, has to sometimes scale a wall before cutting a window or a door off its hinges, using the least amount of time possible of course; this is twice the work a plumber or a fumigator does. A robber cannot hire a mover, for instance; he has to carry the stolen goods all by himself. In any event, later that night the three of us broke into the house, found our colleague and girl sleeping, and one of us started yelling, 'Where's the cat?' because he was already exhausted. I pulled him out of the bedroom and told him to keep calm, we had not come for the cat alone, we were here to perform a robbery; a proper robbery. As far as God was aware that night, we were robbers, I had explained to this gentleman. So we went back into the bedroom and raped the girl, raped his lover, and carried the cat away. One of us said that one of the victims, the man, had identified him. And so we went back into the house and stabbed the girl's lover, left him for dead. He died on his way to the hospital.

"I have since always felt as if we did something, how do I put this, sad, you see, probably because it was on Sunday."

It was a vague feeling, however, probably influenced by my love for my mother, who was against doing any kind of work on Sundays. But the idea of allowing myself to break protocol and allow the girl into the diner way past the closing time had struck me as adequate compensation, as they say. And now I wouldn't have to think about that incident any longer. I could instead focus on how perfectly we played our part that night; take the good from the incident, the pristine, as they call it.

After saying this I sank into my seat once again. She had already sat up, pulling her elbows from the table. We were quiet for a while. Unmoving. I knew I was now free to leave. Her act of pulling away from the table was the signal that she had let go of me. And when I stood she remained sitting still. Unmoving. I said if it was okay with her, I would like to close the diner now. And she rose from the booth slowly like heavy smoke. She stiffly hoisted her pet from the table but did not make any further movement. I asked her to wait as I brought the blinds down because I felt obliged to walk her out. I went into the kitchen and switched off the lights. When I walked from the kitchen she was still standing at the booth. I walked to the door, held it open and after what seemed like a long while she managed to understand that was a signal for her to walk through it, but not before making a painfully slow and almost static walk from the booth. I switched off the lights, closed the door, and walked her now slightly bent frame to her car. After she had started the engine, but not before she had fumbled with her keys at the ignition several times, I tapped at her window (something that startled her) and raised my palm to signal goodbye. The car zigzagged into the B-24 and zoomed off into the night like a stray arrow.

I buttoned up my coat and buried my hands into my pockets and started towards the venue. I had been thinking about my solitary walk all day long, and now I had it. I would walk behind Main Street, past the whorehouse – hoping to catch a glimpse of the prostitutes on the promenade, all depending, and finally into the National Theatre, where a group of writers would be giving readings from their works forty minutes from now. I had been dreading this all day long. I remember once reading *The Master* by Colm Tóibín, where Henry James, out of nervousness, decides to walk instead of sitting in the theatre where his play is premiering.

Literature is filled with writers who spend their time walking. These are difficult times. If you manage to sell one book after giving a reading, you can finally afford to buy a pack of cigarettes to keep you company when you are typing the next story at night, or when you are reading a coverless and tattered copy of *What If I am a Literary Gangster* at the balcony, or when you are simply walking home with one of the half-naked girls at the promenade; what a thing to be able to purchase the love and warmth of a woman's body without having to put up a torturous performance! You can finally afford to employ your mind to other functions than talking.

The Seeds She Grew

Noella Moshi

The day shuffled slowly into twilight, grey and unremarked. Kurwa watched it leave from behind the wooden countertop of Omar's textbook shop, her new job in her new life. A child walked in, clutching his mother's hand with both of his. He stared at Kurwa from behind his mother's skirt, unself-consciously loved. Kurwa smiled at his mother. It had been several months, but large eyes filling small faces still twisted her womb with pain.

Omar's bookshop was on the ground floor of the apartment building where Kurwa now lived, the wires crisscrossing from poles stuck in pavements like overgrown weeds, coating the building with mould and electricity. The child had been the last customer of the day. As Kurwa stepped over the threshold and shut the door behind her, the horns and bicycles ringing outside were a contrast to the muted music of the bookshop. She locked the shop and ascended the stairs to her apartment. It was a low-ceilinged affair: one bedroom and a kitchen. Through the window of her bedroom, Kurwa was steeped in the spicy scent of her neighbours' dinners. She listened to the traffic as she drifted into uneasy sleep. She didn't dream often, but that day she saw the past in her sleep, and it was bathed in the green of her mother's garden. She was its first flower. She grew strange and strong. Uprooted, she was now without the soil that nourished her. Mama would not find her in the maze of crumbling concrete and hard sounds.

*

Years before Kurwa left home, Mama had gazed with crinkly-eyed, bright happiness at her daughters as they walked together through the narrow back-ways of Mbezi, where the world was lush and colourful. Because the footpath behind their house was hidden from the main road, plants were left to decide their size and fate. They lived shorter, grew taller, and reached more boldly toward Mama's striding form. Kurwa and Doto marched behind her, seeing only the backs of her legs, golden-smooth, growing out of cotton shorts. They heard her voice wafting down with stories of each plant as she answered their earnest questions, cooling the stifling humidity with her laughter. The girls halted obediently when Mama noticed an aloe that she wanted for her own garden. She took a cutting, and placed it carefully into her bag.

Kurwa was two years older than Doto, holding her hand as their short, stout legs stepped over branches in pointed black shoes wrapped over white cotton socks. Their hair was stubbornly curly even from the confines of Mama's tightly braided knots.

"Mama, tell us a story!" Kurwa demanded.

Mama took Kurwa's hand as she began. "Story, story," she sang.

"Story come, lies come, tamu colea!" the girls responded in unison.

Mama told them a story of Anansi the Spiderman as the link of three moved in single file along the thin brown line of a path that ended at home.

When they arrived, Mama retrieved the aloe plant from her bag and potted it amidst her jasmine and morning glories. Her garden was terraced, white steps slanting slowly down into a small green valley fringed with frangipani trees.

It was a quiet Sunday, and the breeze mirrored the silence of Mama's slow exhalation as she unbent from her work. She walked briskly back up to the house, already thinking of her preparations for the week ahead: rebraiding each girl's hair in the evening, fixing a batch of mandazi to reheat for Baba's breakfast. First, she would visit Aunty Kekedo, whose husband was not well. She left the girls playing inside and walked to Aunty Kekedo's house.

An hour later, Mama returned to the smell of burning flesh.

"Kurwa!" she yelled from the front door as she hurriedly unlocked the door, chest tightening. "Kurwa, Doto, where are you?"

The girls came running out of their bedroom, where they had been drawing.

Mama dropped to her knees, hugging them close, and they were silent, sensing her anxiety.

Then she straightened up, eyes narrowed.

"What is that smell?"

"Mama, I cooked dinner!" Kurwa offered proudly.

"You did what? I smell burning!" Mama flung open the microwave door to reveal spattered brown pieces of meat coating its roof, and plastic melted onto the microwave plate.

"You spoiled the meat! Kurwa, wait there, wait until I show you how to behave." Mama opened the kitchen drawer and noisily pulled out the wooden spoon she used to stir ugali.

Doto ran behind a dining-room chair to hide.

Kurwa, still secure in her sense of accomplishment, looked bewildered. "Mama, but I cooked for you!"

"You spoiled the kitchen!"

Kurwa's wails ripped open the afternoon silence as she received a beating.

Afterwards, Mama dropped the spoon in the sink and yanked a kitchen cloth from the rail. Before she could move to clean the microwave, Kurwa crawled, still weeping, to wrap her arms around Mama's legs. Mama tried to wrench her off, but Kurwa wouldn't let go.

Kurwa was born speaking a different language to Mama. In the early years, their exchange was a primal codependence, masking the true separation. Later, when Kurwa formed her thoughts separately from Mama's body, they found they could no longer understand each other.

Kurwa found a language that she and Mama could share on the day she carried the offertory at church. Kurwa was wearing a yellow dress and lace-edged socks. Mama had plaited her hair in six pigtails with yellow bows tied at their ends. She walked slowly, like how she had practised at home, the large basket held tightly between her hands. When she handed it over to the priest, she gave a pretty curtsy — she hadn't tried it before, but it seemed right for the moment. She heard chuckles as she returned, flushed, to her seat. Mama put her arm around Kurwa for the remainder of the service, smiling proudly.

After the service, Mama stood with Kurwa to greet neighbours and friends.

Aunty Kekedo squeezed Mama's arm affectionately as she smiled down at Kurwa. "What lovely manners your children have — I wish mine were better mannered!"

Mama was beaming from the attention. When they stepped into the car, she told Baba, "You see, our children have manners — all the aunties were saying so. And they are pretty."

Kurwa didn't understand what manners or looks had to do with the offertory procession. But here was a key to making Mama happy.

Mama and Baba had met at Saint Mary's Secondary School, when Mama was in Form 6. Once they were married, Mama's belly had grown rapidly with Kurwa. The baby was a fleshy distention by exam time. Mama wrote her papers kneeling on the floor of the classroom, sometimes stooping to all fours to ease the weight of her large stomach from her knees. Doto was born a year later.

The first time Baba had seen Mama's golden skin, he had reached out in wonder to brush his fingers against her arm as she walked past.

"*Nini wewe* — What is it?" Mama had turned angrily when she felt his fingers on her arm.

"I'm greeting you. Why are you in such a hurry?" he had replied smilingly.

She'd glared scornfully at him before flouncing away.

The next day Baba drove his car and parked it close to her classroom, just before the end of school. He waited humbly at the stairs of the hall until she emerged.

"Excuse me." He was nervous.

She narrowed her eyes. "You again."

"Yes." He smiled weakly. "I thought that as you are always in a hurry, perhaps I could drive you where you need to go."

She looked past him to the solitary car parked near the building, hesitant.

"Please," he said.

Finally returning his smile, she handed him her school bag and they walked down the stairs together.

Baba proposed because he wanted to study Mama, to understand what made her move gracefully and to think in shapes that his world had no names for. Mama said yes because she was already pregnant with Kurwa.

Mama was proud of her children and her home, but most of all she was proud of her husband's name — a name she had purchased by agreeing to marry him. As a child, illegitimate Mama's hair was shaved off every Sunday to hide her loose, soft curls from scornful eyes at church. Her round head, oddly large on her thin neck, stood unself-consciously straight as she sat with the other children, luminous yellow amidst the sea of brown. When Mama turned seven, her mother moved her to the back room of Aunty Marushe's house, where she learnt how to cook food for Aunty's husband and three children, whom she did not like to play with. Aunty continued the tradition of shaving Mama's head on Sundays, smirking as she rubbed oil into Mama's scalp afterwards. For Mama, marriage was a bid for a seat in the front rooms of the same relatives' homes.

When Kurwa was born, the relatives came flooding into Mama and Baba's front room. Mama savoured the rap-rapping of aunties' knuckles on the door, the clinking of teacups, the tittering exchange of gossip. The past was ironed out under gifts of kangas and wedding invitations. Mama, with her too-light skin and too-soft hair, was now family to those who had made her their children's servant. Even Aunty Marushe visited. Middle-aged, she had fat, rolling chins and dark elbows where she forgot to bleach her skin. Mama sent for soda and arranged mandazi on a plate for Aunty Marushe. They sat sipping and chewing to conceal the silence of memory. Aunty rocked Kurwa, jowls wobbling as she pronounced approvingly: "She looks like her father."

Mama would remember those first days of motherhood later, when Kurwa's name was no longer spoken at Mbezi, and the relatives opened their back rooms once more.

In those first years, Kurwa was happy too. She and Doto followed Mama as she wove her way through chores, squabbles, and birthday parties — moments slipped by in a haze of contentment. At the clothes warehouse, where they shopped for second-hand clothes — rejects from the US and the UK — Kurwa paused to look through the open door of the darkened room to where the plants jostled to reach beyond painted yellow lines of concrete, creating a scraggly horizon for the clear blue sky. A warm waft of air played with her frizzy hair. She closed her eyes and wet her lips to taste the sunlight as it glanced off stacks of old books.

Everything changed when Kurwa's body shifted into womanhood. Her skin became glistening honey, and her eyes were cut with eager intelligence. Her long legs ended in thin ankles, making her movements seem both precarious and urgent. Days of sleepy idyll were no longer enough for her. She couldn't describe what she was looking for, only that it compelled her to write poems about missing limbs. She wrote almost every night before bedtime, scribbling secretively in a blue diary she kept under her mattress, a gift from Baba on her thirteenth birthday.

"Baby, let's have a party and invite your friends to the house for your birthday." Mama smiled at her daughter in the mirror as she braided Kurwa's hair into cornrows.

It was dusk, a week before Kurwa turned thirteen. Doto was outside kicking a soccer ball in the small grass patch at the front of the house. The sound of the evening news could be heard from the living room, where Baba was seated, Serengeti beer on the coffee table next to him.

"No, Mama. You know I hate parties."

"But why, baby? I haven't seen your friends in a while; you are always by yourself in your room, and it's not good. You need to exercise too, you know."

"I'm not fat, Ma."

"I didn't say that, baby, but it's not good for you to stay by yourself all the time."

Kurwa stared balefully at her mother's reflection. "Stop bugging me about this, okay? I don't want one."

Mama shifted on her feet, glancing wordlessly at Kurwa in the mirror before she picked up the next section of hair to braid.

Mama was afraid of this new Kurwa, with her moody silence and cagey restlessness. Kurwa's words were fewer, her laughs shorter. Sometimes when white morning light streamed through Mama's curtain, she saw six-year-old Kurwa again, standing in the doorframe, one hand resting on the wood. Then loneliness ached Mama's teeth and she struggled not to call out. Where was her child? Her mind arrived at fearful conclusions: sex, disease, and babies without names. She said nothing directly to Kurwa, but could be heard preaching loudly from the kitchen about fallen women — Zawadi, who was raped because she spoke to a stranger; Bahati, who fell in love with a married man and now cried herself to sleep; and Rehema, pregnant and disowned. At first Kurwa listened, but when Mama's stories began to sound the same, she ignored them.

Kurwa saw Mama's worried glances, but was helpless to explain that it was not the stretch marks over her buttocks, or the hair growing in new places that she was afraid of. It was the sense that there was something beyond her current life that she must grasp. She was afraid because she knew that she must have it, and that it would change her.

"Ma!" Kurwa's feet thumped on the wooden floors of the house as she ran from her bedroom to the living room. "Ma, did you touch my diary?" Kurwa's eyes were wild as she stopped abruptly in front of the kitchen counter where Mama was rolling dough for chapati, and thrust the journal under Mama's nose.

Mama's face was carefully expressionless as she looked back at Kurwa. "Kurwa, it's my right as your mother to know what's going on in your life."

Kurwa's voice trembled as she squeezed out three words: "How dare you?"

"Eh, you are writing strange things, a child like you shouldn't be thinking about!" Mama dropped the rolling pin violently on the counter. "You should be ashamed, writing such things!"

Kurwa looked at Mama, her eyes hard. "I will never trust you again."

"I'm your mother. You cannot talk to me like that!" Mama's voice held the shrill ring of panic.

Kurwa stormed back into her room, slamming her door behind her. Mama, hands shaking slightly, continued to roll the chapati.

That night Kurwa woke before sunrise, her abdomen contracting in pain. Nausea bubbled up her throat from warm, thick blood between her legs. Her fingers curled tightly around her bed sheet — she was scared but she didn't want to ask Mama for help. Instead, she filled the bathtub with scalding water and eased herself into it, fighting the pulsing fear digging into her uterus. She counted pinpricks of sensation while watching dawn break from behind the small bathroom window. Blood escaped in liquid crimson puffs from between her legs, and she felt empty.

Saturday was always grocery-shopping day. Mama's chiding pushed a sullen Kurwa into the car with Doto. Kurwa's lips were squashed into a thin, pinched line, her arms crossed tightly over her chest. When they park outside the grocery store, she threw up, her stomach cramped into dizzying pain.

Mama held Kurwa to steady her, eyes squinting with worry. "Baby, what did you eat?"

Kurwa shook her head and moved away from Mama to sit back in the car. Mama followed her.

"What's wrong?"

Kurwa rested her head on the seat, and still did not speak.

"Let's go to the clinic today. It might be malaria."

Kurwa was goaded to speak by her hate of the clinic, with its lines of silently waiting people and the ringing smell of disinfectant. "Mama, I'm bleeding," she said in a dull voice.

"Okay," Mama replied, looking around to make sure no one heard. "Keep your voice down about such things. Stay in the car. I'll buy you some pads."

After some minutes in the car, Kurwa felt better, but bored. She followed Mama and Doto into the supermarket. Before she could find them, she saw a man — perhaps in his forties — staring at her through a gap in the shelves. He watched her boldly, as if he could see through her clothes. Yellow eyeballs filled his thin face. She could make out a browning collar and buttoned shirt tucked into a black plastic belt. Kurwa became uncomfortable and curious. She stared back at him, moving closer, matching his naked scrutiny. Suddenly, a hand shot out between the shelves to squeeze her left breast. Kurwa, startled, pushed his hand from her and hurried away.

That night Kurwa dreamt that she was shedding burning skin, stretching it to shreds, as she grew taller. In her dream, her flat chest itched painfully. She scratched compulsively, watching her skin peel back under the pressure of twin mounds, fleshy quivering extensions of skinless breasts. She woke breathing heavily, afraid of the mystery.

Perhaps it was Mama's fear that spurred Kurwa to search for answers in a boy; perhaps it was inevitable. He saw her first at the kibanda where she bought airtime. He was leaning on a wooden post, watching her scratch a voucher. His brown feet were dusty in their sandals and sweat droplets patterned his upper lip. His gaze made the hair on her arms stand up. She refused to return it.

Finally, he spoke, "My name is Ombeni. We should be friends." The authority in his voice surprised Kurwa. He looked older, but not by much. His smile seemed secretive.

"I'm Kurwa," she responded, "and I have enough friends."

He smiled again. "Not friends like me."

In the evening, she led him into Mama's garden, where she picked unripe lemons from the short lemon tree, her bare feet drinking the cool grass, and her lips hoping to touch his. They sat on the steps while Mama and Baba were at prayer group, Doto keeping a lookout for them from the house. Kurwa listened intently to her body as Ombeni moved nearer, noting the startling flushes across her chest, the sweat on her palms. When he spoke, she furtively touched his arm. His skin bulged with tight muscle.

Ombeni leaned closer, and Kurwa pulled back, suddenly more scared than curious. But it was too late. He pressed himself against her, and she felt her flesh yield against the hard muscles of his torso. Their first kiss made his words more urgent. Despite being unmoved by his lust-laced flattery, Kurwa allowed him to speak, hoping that eventually he would tell her about herself.

The first time Kurwa and Ombeni had sex was quick and uncomfortable, a pushed-up coupling behind a mango tree. It was a Sunday afternoon, so Mama and Baba were visiting neighbours, and Doto had dozed off on the balcony. Afterwards, Kurwa recalled the feel of bark against her buttocks; the unbroken trail of black ants a scribble on the ground, and his absorbed grunting. She stared in open wonder at Ombeni's contorted face, his eyes partially closed in concentration.

Kurwa didn't enjoy the sharp thrusting sensation, and was repulsed by Ombeni's blankness. He did not know her. She was not his. But to stop him would be to admit that it was not enough; that she had hoped life would be more impressive than this. Her disappointment remained an unacknowledged ache.

As a child, Kurwa had been convinced that the moon followed her around. Whenever she turned, there it was, drifting lazily through clouds, looking down at her, proof of her uniqueness. When she found out the moon was unfaithfully trailing after Doto as well, it was her first real heartbreak.

When Ombeni was done, Kurwa pulled up her shorts and tried to answer his searching face with a reassuring smile. But she was so tired. She walked slowly back into the house. He let himself out of the garden quietly.

Mama noticed Kurwa gaining weight uniformly, her widened arms and legs softening the shock of her growing belly, but said nothing. Kurwa stopped getting her period. Only Doto saw the hidden stash of pads accumulating in the shoe cupboard. She heard Kurwa's muted sobs in the darkness of their bedroom, and was afraid.

Nine months later, and for a second time that year, Kurwa woke before sunrise. There was a dull ache in her lower back and a pressure on her pelvis.

Mama woke too, spurred by some impulse from her womb. She got out of bed quietly, leaving Baba snoring, and tiptoed into her daughters' room. Mama saw the soft rise and fall of Doto's sleeping form, but Kurwa's bed was empty. Heart racing, she padded quietly to the bathroom. The door was shut but not locked. She opened it and entered.

Mama saw her daughter as if for the first time. Kurwa on the bathtub ledge, her underwear flung beneath the bathroom sink, fluid dripping between her opened legs. Her hands were holding something between her thighs. Kurwa's dampened skin shone power into the room. Her jaw, clamped shut against the pain, manifested supreme control.

Was this her child?

Mama averted her gaze; at first fearing that the baby was dead, and then fearing it was alive. The baby slipped out while Mama was cleaning a pair of scissors under the tap. She knelt in front of her daughter, and cut the umbilical chord. Mama sat on the floor holding the child in her arms, its pink face scrunched. She looked up at her daughter's tired face and whispered entreatingly, "Let it be mine."

Mama had moved like water through life. She became a niece, a wife, a mother, fitting into whatever shape her container demanded. When she saw Kurwa giving birth, Mama felt with her own body that possession disguised as love was still brutal. Yet, holding this child, Mama could no longer understand herself without it. Already she knew the shape of its fingers and the pace of its blood. Here, for Mama, was a fresh chance to buckle pointed black shoes, wrapped over white cotton socks. She was lost in this child's softness.

Dawn broke before Mama tore herself away from the child to look again at Kurwa. Sadness to Mama would from then on be the image of Kurwa, slumped in an empty tub, her brown eyes small and buried in her swollen face. Kurwa was young again, and Mama had just smacked her, and Kurwa was waiting to be held.

"I'll clean the child up, Kurwa." Mama's voice was steady. "You go on back to bed."

In the months after the child was born, Kurwa was allowed to breastfeed the child in secret. Her face was soft only in the moments before Mama took the child away again, a ritualistic reenactment of the first time. Kurwa was becoming someone else, someone she had to be. Her mind grew cave-like, and her thoughts fusty. She coated her eyes in dark war paint, layering red lipstick onto tightly pressed lips. She lied smoothly at church about whose child Mama held, and the neighbours pretended to believe her.

"The baby is growing fast!" Aunty Kekedo cooed as she stroked its cheek.

The baby was nestled in blankets, eyes closed, rocking in Mama's arms. Kurwa, Doto and Mama were seated on their regular pew, receiving greetings. Kurwa's fists were clenched in her lap. She had vague notions of leaving Mbezi, but she didn't know where to go. She was seventeen now, a number that rung like the sound of pens being dropped in an exam room.

At 6pm on Sunday, Baba switched the television to the news as he had done every day for the past twenty years. Kurwa heard the opening music from outside as she sat on the grass, watching the twilight turn into night. The street was silent except for the echo of TV music, broadcasting the death of another day. So when Mama suggested Kurwa move out, just for a while, so that the child didn't become confused about whom her mother was, Kurwa readily agreed.

As Mama lay in bed that night, she thought about her girls and her flowers, in wonder at the bold ambition it took to raise them. She twitched in her settling sleep. She wanted to show Kurwa how glory hides in the mundane — to tell her not to dig for seeds that must be left to grow – but she couldn't speak any more, and besides, Kurwa was gone.

The Story Not Told

Acidri Malunga

October 1975. The rickety cargo plane taxied unsteadily on the runway of Lagos airport amidst a torrential downpour, jolting me out of my drunken stupor. The UN officer next to me wiped the little streams of sweat flowing out of his coal-dark hair with the back of a chubby hand, and let out a weary sigh. He turned to me and said a brief hello, as if I had suddenly appeared next to him. I nodded back my hello with a plastic smile, and at once determined that his silence throughout the five-hour flight was a better act of courtesy for the blast of foul air that accompanied his greeting was more sickening than the humid conditions just outside our rusty capsule.

I was in Nigeria for my doctoral dissertation in literature, and my area of research was on the contribution of native writers to the rise of contemporary African literature. My first stop was the little village of Umuofia, immortalised by its son Chinua Achebe in his literary masterpieces. A row of tin-roofed, mud-and-wattle structures welcomed me into what I later came to learn was the trading centre. Just behind this commercial hub, as I turned off the dirt road and into an alley that led to an expanse of grassland, goats and sheep were munching on coarse grass. A young man, who wore a faint moustache and who croaked when he spoke, serenaded a voluptuous village belle with a rendition of Shakespearean romance.

"Uhmm... hello, boss," I mumbled, with the best humility I could muster. One of the lessons I had learnt in my many years of lecturing literature at Makerere University was the power of validating young people; their esteem, their feelings, their whole being. If you came across as friendly and nonjudgmental, you could get pretty much anything out of them — these youngsters.

The young man cast a vexed look in my direction, pushing out his muscular chest like a cobra intimidating its prey. His lover instinctively knelt down and mumbled a greeting in Ibo. I replied with a loving smile, and seized the moment to squeeze out some juice.

"My boss here is a very lucky man to have a beautiful *anyaka* like you."

At this, the young man's tough countenance softened into a shy smile and he asked what *anyaka* meant.

"*Anyaka* is the name of a beautiful young girl. As you can guess by now, I am not from these parts. Actually, I am from Uganda — the land of Amin. I came here to hear the stories of the land from the storytellers themselves, for I believe Chinua Achebe — God bless him — is not the only good storyteller in these parts."

My point hit home. The young man broke into a bout of hearty laughter — the laughter of a man whose spirit brimmed with pride at the tickle of their ego.

"I know," he offered in between fits of laughter and chest thumping. "A couple for sure, starting with myself." The aura of self-importance with which he made the offer sounded more like an effort to score points with the object of his affections, and not genuine assistance one would give a bespectacled gentleman on an intellectual quest.

I politely declined, whereupon he suggested three elders whom he said were revered in Umofia and beyond for their storytelling prowess. The first of these was one Maduka, custodian of the Ibo Cultural Center. I found his name strangely familiar.

The two lovebirds led me to Maduka's homestead, hand in hand, the belle giggling at what seemed to be a session of beautiful storytelling from the self-proclaimed orator. I galloped along, my old bones hardly keeping up with the spring in the steps of the two youths. After a mile or so, we branched into a neatly swept compound that hosted five large grass-thatched huts.

The gentleman I was introduced to was a well-built fellow in the prime of his life, whose hair was surprisingly sprinkled with a fair portion of grey. As my hand hang limp in his firm grip, my guide quickly pointed out that the man I was meeting was one of the wisest and most respected elders in the whole of Umuofia. As if to emphasise the point, the young man kissed Maduka's foot and politely excused himself from our company.

I took that as my cue to stop staring at my host's bizarre constitution and accord him the expected respect.

After we had exchanged pleasantries over kola nuts and palm wine, I broached the reason for my visit in the broadest terms possible – these people were not the kind you rush, however urgent your cause might be. If I had visited him at the centre perhaps we might have had an academic discussion, but seeing as it is that I had come to his home, we were going to have one long conversation.

"Maduka, my brother, I believe you are familiar with this," I said, waving a copy of *Things Fall Apart* in my left hand. "At least your namesake is somewhere in here."

My host eased into his seat with the same indifferent expression his face had assumed after I introduced myself as a lecturer of literature on a research mission. At length, he spoke.

"Maduka, son of Obierika. That is what's written in the book you are holding. Much of what I wish to tell you is not written in that book. I believe if all you wanted were in that book, you wouldn't have taken the pains to travel this far through stream and strife. Am I right?"

I nodded.

"Listen. I wish to tell you something rather confidential. It may or may not be of help to your doctoral studies but I will tell you nonetheless. Don't ask me why of all people I choose to share this with you, for I also don't know why. Sometimes you dislike someone at first sight. Sometimes you like them. Sometime you find it most reassuring to trust a complete stranger."

Again, I nodded.

"It has been written that Okwonkwo committed suicide after killing a court messenger. He hanged himself." Maduka gave me a piercing look as though there was anything mystical about what he had just said.

"Sure... that's obvious..." I stammered, quite startled by the awkward turn our conversation had taken. "I could read to you the last page of the book."

"Wrong," he whispered, seemingly afraid that the lazy dog lounging at his feet may recognise the cat he was about to let out of his weather-beaten bag. He kicked the poor creature and it let out a startled howl before limping off to the cool shade of a granary a couple of feet away.

I reclined back in my seat, bracing for a waste of my precious time by a native. I nudged him on with a feigned interest, if only to get him to speak his gibberish and allow me to leave his damned company.

"Wrong," he repeated. "That young man wrote that to shield his father from the masters he had chosen to serve. He was torn between loyalty to his father — and by extension the land of his forefathers on one hand, and a strong conviction that the white man brought true justice to his people, on the other."

I noticed where he seemed to be heading and quickly interrupted him.

"Do you mean to say...?" Words failed me. My quickness of comprehension had not translated into a quickness of articulation. My host nodded knowingly.

"The world knows him as Chinua Achebe, but around here, he is simply known as Nwoye — Okwonkwo's first son. Nwoye the lazy boy. Nwoye the learned one. Nwoye the prodigal son."

Confused, I listened, no longer sure whether this fellow was wasting my time or was drawing back the veil on a virgin tale.

"Chinua Achebe told the story of his grandfather Unoka, whom popular legend says he took after in laziness and in art; he told the story of his father Okwonkwo, whom he found too brute to be human; and his own story, which was a conflict of all three pulling in different directions. That was the story he tried to tell in *Things Fall Apart*. By and large he told the truth, except that he conveniently excluded certain details at the very end to keep his father off the white man's noose. *No Longer at Ease* came much later, because it was an observation of his own son's life."

"Tell me more about *Things Fall Apart*," I demanded, my patience waring thin.

"Achebe left his readers in suspense with the discovery of his father's hanging body, and the popular presumption is that Okwonkwo died. To the readers, this was a tragedy. To the colonial establishment, this was a major victory in the endeavor to pacify the primitive tribes of the lower Niger delta — as they preferred to call us. Perhaps you may not know, but *Things Fall Apart* was initially written as a post-mortem report under the hand of one Dr Keith, a young intern doctor who sympathised with the African struggle and had formed a close friendship with Achebe himself.

"The report was one sentence long, contained in the last page of the book, and was simply a statement that death had been probably caused by strangulation. Achebe simply adapted it as a creative story because he was born a great storyteller, but more importantly, to find a preoccupation for the clueless white men who, more than desiring to subjugate the black man, sought to understand his peculiar ways.

"But it was not whole. And the missing bit of the story is what I wish to tell you."

I listened, the environment around us suddenly turning so serene that a simple mind would gladly attribute this to the sense of the occasion. Even the wind rustling the surrounding tree leaves seemed to have stopped by to eavesdrop.

"After he beheaded the lead court messenger, Okwonkwo did not go to his home. He came to see my father — for as any keen reader may be aware — they were the best of friends. It is true that he intended to take his life with his own hands rather than be hanged like a rabid dog in the market square by those colonial officers and their *agbala* messengers. He wasn't prepared to flee either, for his ego would not have the very thought of a second exile.

"Being the thoughtful man he was, my father reclined in his seat and was quiet for almost an hour, even though Okwonkwo's nerves nearly fell apart. It was palm wine that kept him contained. At long last my father spoke: 'You will not be hanged by them, and neither will you do it with your hand. I will do it for you,' my father whispered with suppressed excitement, to the consternation of all those present — Okwonkwo, my two mothers and myself. 'Here are some *Ogbuefi* roots. Maduka will pound them into a fine powder and you will inhale it like snuff. It will kill you, without sending you six feet under. That way, your body will go into such a deep slumber that your heart will barely see reason to labour. I don't know how much will achieve the desired result but, like our forefathers said, a drowning man is wise in clutching onto straw.'

"So when I arrived with a small bowl of the powdery stuff, my father took a pinch and asked the mighty Okwonkwo to look at the lone *nza* hovering above in the clear skies. The fugitive complied, lifting his chin as if he was on the lookout for any dark clouds heralding his impending doom. My father sprinkled the stuff into both airways, each large enough for a nymph to crawl in and out without much ado. Within the blink of an eye, a solemn serenity descended upon Okwonkwo, and he was as good as dead.

"I was sent out to mobilise a couple of young men to rush to Okwonkwo's homestead with an intention of verifying rumors that he had killed himself. Father gave me a specific instruction not to let any of the villagers in on the conspiracy, for in such desperate times you cannot tell who is for you or against you. Even his family was not filled in on the secret, and it was agreed that the vegetating hero shall be delivered by way of the bush behind his compound. In any case, even our own Nwoye had cut himself out as a disciple of the enemies of Umuofia. I was to join the rest at Okwonkwo's homestead.

"When I got to Okwonkwo's homestead, some of the men I informed first had already arrived and it seemed as though my father had freshly broken the news to the family, for the blooming beauty Ezinma was weeping in my old man's chest, while Nwoye sat under his father's hut. Although he was clearly absent in spirit, he was present nonetheless. Whispers and awkward stares directed at him bespoke of suspicion at the prospect of having a spy in our midst, but that was not pursued any further. He was present. That said a lot.

"To this day, I can't get my head around what degree of clandestine efficiency my father and his nameless, faceless accomplices used but on good authority I have it that he walked into his friend's compound through the courtyard to break the tragic news, while four demons effected the tragedy without causing an actual tragedy in the backyard. Before I could even seat my swampy butt next to my age mate Nwoye, a giant pig on two legs was led into Okwonkwo's compound escorted by an armed band of black boys.

"He marched about with such an air of self-importance that I could not help but chuckle at the irony of it all. His flittering eyes collided with my bemused own, and his snout knitted into a look of utmost contempt. I quickly imagined my own father being castrated by this strange creature — such stories were not unheard of those days — just so that my face could assume a semblance of seriousness. Even hate.

"'Which of you bears the name Okwonkwo?' the colonial officer grunted, his baritone strongly laced with animosity.

"No one in the compound found the question worth answering. Except my father. He led the white man slowly around Okwonkwo's obi, taking his sweet time to get there as though he wanted to buy time for his accomplices at work. When they got around to the crime scene, my old man heaved a sigh of relief. The sight was rather heart wrenching — picture perfect for those who knew better. Okwonkwo hanged from a *jalof* tree by a cow rope, rather peculiar because any villager in these parts would know for a fact that this is a rather slow, unsure way to die.

"One of the court messengers was instructed by the white fellow to cut down the body, while his colleagues supported it from below. He was laid to rest on the bare ground as Nwoye came around the corner to cast a final look at the father he had rejected. For no apparent reason, one of the court messengers struck Okwonkwo in the genitalia with the butt of his gun. There was a low groan from the corpse and everyone took an instinctive step backwards. A patch of wet issued forth from the white man's own, and we couldn't tell whether it was because of a fear of the dead or the fear of pain. But fear was registered all the same.

"And then all hell broke loose.

"Nwoye, indifferent this whole time, set the fire. He grabbed my father's walking stick and struck at the court messenger who had thus disgraced his father, the blow landing squarely at the base of his neck. He collapsed in a heap, without a sound. In a fit of panic, a few aimless shots were fired, and everyone scampered for safety. When a semblance of peace seemed to return, the white pig lay bleeding at the foot of a well-built hulk of a man, whose face writhed somewhat in agony, and the awkward part of his legs told of a burning sensation where life issued from.

"One of the armed escorts took aim at Okwonkwo, but was thrown off balance by a rock hurled at the side of his head by an unknown assailant. Okwonkwo grabbed the gun and those who knew his perfect record with misfired shots ducked for dear life.

"There was a loud boom, a plume of smoke and a dead man. A second one. A third one. A fourth. And his cartridges were exhausted.

"Umuofia at once recognised the enemy Okwonkwo had been fighting this whole time. It was not the white pig or his ilk that he had a bone to pick with. The enemy was much closer than previously thought. The terrified soldiers and messengers took to their heels, and the bellicose Umuofians followed them in hot pursuit. Sure enough, they were captured and dragged back to the battle scene, dripping with blood from a fair dose of mob justice.

"Before it was decided which punishment was best suited for them, Nwoye was sent off to the mission to sell to the big men a version of events closer to truth than lie: Their white colleague had been shot dead by his escorts during a spontaneous revolt at a stubborn resister's funeral. They had been arrested and would be put to death for desecrating life. That was the way of the land, and the white man sure had no trouble with local cultures where they furthered his interests. In any case, this would somewhat confirm that the locals were beginning to cooperate with the establishment. Nwoye knew his masters well, but also knew himself better now. He was *a man of the people.*

"And from such events, simple as they were mysterious, a struggle was born. A struggle of the Ibo people to free themselves not from the embrace of alien men, but from the grip of their brothers from distant villages. Kinsmen who merely used the coming of the white man to override the prowess of Umuofia. This is the story of Biafra."

Maduka reclined in his seat and took a gulp of palm wine. He gave me a satisfied smile and then added, "You are the first man to have been told the full account of events, outside the circle of actors. Do me a favor; tell this story to the whole world, picking up from where Nwoye left off in *Things Fall Apart.* But don't tell it now, for we do not know how the struggle for Biafra will pan out. We are outgunned, outnumbered and outmaneuvered. We are also tired of the war.

"Okwonkwo, though old and frail, remains at the helm of this struggle. He lives in our midst, under an alias. Nwoye is currently in America, mobilising for the cause. He has no plans of returning anytime soon, but he asked me to get the story out when he goes to meet Unoka and the others. Only get this story to the world after the struggle has been finally determined, and after Okwonkwo and his son, the lad you prefer to call Chinua Achebe, have departed to the world of peace and rest and happiness."

The impact of the story was such that I was temporarily immobilised. I didn't know what next to say, except to ask the lame question, "Who are you?"

"I am Maduka, son of Obierika. That much should be clear in the book you are holding."

"And why should I believe your story?" I fired back.

"Ezinma! Ezinma-oo!" Maduka called out.

A beautiful lady came out of the smoke bellowing hut and knelt respectfully besides him. Maduka stroked her hair lovingly, and she smiled with the shyness of a newlywed bride.

"This is my wife Ezinma. She is also – and more importantly for you – the daughter of Okwonkwo himself. She hasn't heard a thing of what I just told you. Cross check with her – she has my permission to share. And if you still aren't convinced, I permit her to lead you to her father himself and to write to her brother Nwoye in America. Would there be greater proof than that?"

And so it came to be that, one after the other, I verified the story with the protagonists in the book *Things Fall Apart* and the account was consistent.

To date, no research or dissertation has done a better job of telling this story than my work from that excursion. Yet, my greatest pride was not in graduating top of my doctoral class. Rather, it was the secret Maduka entrusted me to share with the world, a secret of a story not told.

The Way of His Heart

Kouadio Kouakou

Translated from French, *La voie de son coeur*,

by Edwige-Renée Dro

Sitting on a hospital bench with his hands around his head, Hamed was thinking. For a few days now, that is what he has been doing.

How could he have done that to his father?

Why such a disavowal?

He arrived at this hospital two weeks ago and it was then they diagnosed him with lung cancer. He'd promised himself to follow to the letter the advice of the doctor, but soon, he'd gone back to his old ways. Seeing the doctor today approach him, the words spoken to him during his last visit came back to him, amplified.

"For the sake of your health, Mr Hamed, you must stop drinking and smoking."

Hamed had been expecting admonitions but with a little smile, he told Hamed, "I'll be with you in a little while."

He'd barely left when Hamed saw a dark-skinned woman with a child by her side. He almost jumped off the bench and his heart started beating wildly. He shouted. "Lydia!"

She did not reply. He called a second time, and a third time. Still, no response.

What if it isn't Lydia?

He used all the strength he had to get up and in a short while, he reached the woman. He grabbed her by the shoulder and she turned around. Hamed was embarrassed when he saw that it wasn't Lydia.

"I'm sorry."

Making his way back to the bench, his thoughts turned to Lydia.

It was three years ago when Lydia and her family arrived in Myan, his clean and brightly-lit city. Beautiful and always smiling, there was no curse word to be found on her lips. She was the daughter every parent wanted to have. Like every young man his age, Hamed wanted to attract the attention of the young girl. Like every young man, he wanted to have her, forgetting however, that he wasn't like the others. Or at least, that he didn't have a father like his friends had.

Hamed's father was the Imam of the mosque and the spiritual guide of the Muslim community of Myan. Imam Konaté did not remarry after the death of his wife Mariam, arguing that he was too old to fulfil his conjugal duties. He'd therefore raised his six children by himself, five girls, and Hamed, the only boy. He loved them, and they also loved him.

On the first day of Ramadan, he'd been walking past his father's bedroom, Imam Konaté had beckoned Hamed to come in. The room was tastefully decorated. Beautiful paintings from the Holy Land adorned the walls. A beautiful carpet, most likely of the same origin as the paintings, lay on the floor. After looking at Hamed for what seemed like an eternity, his father spoke.

"My son, I'm no longer in my prime, and things are not how they used to be. You're the only son Allah gave me. As such, you have the daunting task to uphold the family name. Your sisters will get married and will have to leave home and go and build their own homes. I'm relying on your faith in Allah and in his prophet. My wish is that you become an Imam. You will be an example of piety, of determination and of faith to many. Will you do me that honour?"

A few years ago, Hamed would have said yes without any hesitation. But there was that girl Lydia, who'd started to turn his head to the point of making him lose sleep. Every day, he passed by her house in the hope of seeing her and hear her reply to his greeting.

A violent fall snapped Hamed out of his reverie.

Allah! He shouted, and felt the ground for the thing that caused his fall. It was a toy a little boy had left lying around. In that hospital bustling with people, every eye turned towards him. But his thoughts were to Allah and on how he'd turned his back on Him to take another way: the way of his heart.

During Ramadan, as always, every member of the Konaté family invited friends to share a meal. That event had brought a lot of pleasure to everyone, but Hamed's joy had been far bigger. The youngest sister had invited Lydia and seeing her arrive at their home that evening with his sister had almost made Hamed trip over. Her dark skin highlighted by the navy blue dress she wore, had left him speechless.

While his father was busy seeing some friends off, Lydia approached him.

"I've been in this neighbourhood for a while but we've never had the chance to talk. I'm Lydia. Lydia Koffi."

"I know." Hamed had replied.

"Oh really! How?"

"Myan is a little town. Everyone knows everyone here, and news travels."

"I take it that you're Hamed. Your sister often talks to me about you."

"About?"

"Nothing in particular. We girls talk about a lot of unimportant things."

Their talk had lasted a few minutes during which she asked him what his goals were.

"To tell you the truth, I hardly give it a thought. I think however that I only want to serve God."

"Meaning?"

"Becoming an Imam."

He read the surprise that showed on her face, but the party was coming to an end and the time for prayers was getting close.

Once he finished praying, Hamed went over his day. Mosque. A meal with his family. And that visit from Lydia, which had been a surprise.

Damn! I forgot to ask her for her number.

But he didn't have to wait too long to have it. Taking a seat next to him on the sofa, his younger sister Katy skilfully slid him a folded piece of paper. On that piece of paper, was written Lydia's number.

From then on, they were on the phone from Monday to Sunday. Once, during one of their conversations, she'd asked whether he really wanted to become an Imam. He'd replied without much conviction that he was passionate about the vocation, and he also wanted to please his father. Deep down however, Hamed had known that Lydia had touched a sensitive chord.

Once Ramadan was over, Lydia started becoming a regular in the Konaté household, and she often wore seductive clothes.

Days went by.

Lydia was seducing and Hamed was falling under her spell.

His father was observing how little by little, Hamed started swapping his usual boubous for Jeans and T-shirts.

His father continued to observe.

To the call of the muezzin, he responded less and less. His father worried. He started neglecting the Holy Book for people magazines.

His father became outraged.

"My son, what's the matter? For some time now, you haven't been to prayers. Your clothing has changed. All this to impress a girl. A servant of Allah, a good Muslim, should not forsake his God for just any old woman. Remember what I have often told you. The headship of this family, and that of this mosque as well, lie on your shoulders. Life, my son, is not smooth for a young man like you."

With his head bowed, Hamed had barely been able to look his father in the eye. The Imam had continued.

"You have feelings and I can't do anything about them, but you are a servant of Allah. Can you imagine how disgraced I will be if the son of the Imam was turning away from his destiny to take another way? Or, if he allowed his head to be turned by a woman! I will no longer be able to walk in this town with my head held high. What kind of advice would I give to these young people who come seeking me out every day?"

Hamed had felt his father on the verge of tears. He was almost crying. The words he spoke broke into Hamed and brought out of him questions. His father left the room with his head bowed. Alone at least, he had been able to think on everything his father told him.

Why did he want to be an Imam? Out of duty or out of love? And Lydia, why did she choose him out of so many suitors? Could he convince her to choose Islam for herself?

From that moment, nothing was as before. On one hand, religion and his family. On the other, Lydia and her beauty.

Hamed started to become a regular in the clubs and the other hot spots of the town despite his father's admonitions. Cigarettes and alcohol became his favourite pastimes. His father, whom shock had rendered mute, could only look at him with disapproving eyes. Some young Muslims thought that he'd lost his mind while others saw him as a hero.

A year later, his sister Katy told him that Lydia wasn't well and she'd even thrown up in the toilets of a shop. Lydia was pregnant. Hamed's sisters knew this. His friends as well. Lydia's parents too.

Hamed's father also knew. Everyone, but him. His lack of experience had made him unable to see the changes in the young woman's body. To him, her migraines and vomiting were just passing discomforts. He explained away her frequent stomach aches as women's problems.

Not long after this, while he was sprawled on the sofa watching TV, a huge man burst into the room. Lydia and her mother, were beside him.

"Who is he?" The man shouted.

With her head bowed, Lydia pointed to Hamed.

"You've lost your tongue?" He shouted. "Tell me who got you pregnant?"

The noise woke up the Imam, who had been sleeping in his room.

"Good evening, Sir. What's going on? Why are you making all this noise in my house?"

"You really want to know what's going on? Well, ask your son. I haven't come here to make a speech but only to let you know that from today, this girl that your son knows very well, will live here. She's not my child anymore, she is yours now."

Lydia's mother was holding her husband by his arm as if she wanted to prevent him from doing something from which there would be no coming back. Hamed turned towards Lydia.

Could he deny being the author of this pregnancy?

The evidence was there before him. Lydia's stomach had taken on some proportions. When the ambassador and his wife left the house, Hamed's father fell down in an armchair with his hands over his eyes and shook his head. Imam Konate let his tears flow. Ashamed, Lydia stood like a statue by the door. As for Hamed, he just wanted to disappear.

Lydia's father stayed true to his threat. Lydia remained in the Konaté household. Many a times, Hamed's father sought to see her parents, to no avail. As for Hamed, his father stopped giving him anything. Neither greetings, nor money. Hamed wandered around town in order to have something with which to look after Lydia, but alcohol and cigarettes ate all the money he managed to earn. Returning home one evening, he noticed that Lydia wasn't there, but he did not worry. Maybe she'd gone to town, he told himself.

But when his father called him into his room, it was a man with a glowing face, a face that he hadn't seen since the day Lydia's father came in to do his number. He'd barely sat down when his father started.

"When Allah closes a door, he opens another one. Just as day replaces night, grievances can be replaced by joy and happiness."

Hamed did not know where his father was going with his speech.

What was he on about? Had Lydia had the baby? But how could that be possible when she was only 6 months' pregnant?

"Lydia's mother, that Madam Koffi, she came here this morning. She apologises for her husband's behaviour. She asked to go home with her daughter, something which I didn't find any inconvenience to. My son, I think we need to let them look after their daughter and the baby."

Hamed had not waited to hear the end of that sentence; he was already at the door.

His father shouted after him.

"If you step over the threshold of that door, you will no longer step foot into this house. Here is your opportunity to get your life back, and get back to your destiny. If you step out of this house, consider that I am no longer your father."

Hamed stopped but for a moment before he ran out. In a few minutes, he was in front of the Koffi household. He rang the bell, again and again, but no-one answered. He would have climbed the wall had it not been for the size of it. He sat in front of the gate and cried. His heart bled. But more so when the warder who'd come to get his belongings told him that Lydia and her family had left for

Europe.

He'd lost Lydia. He'd lost his family. He even told himself that Allah was far from him.

His friends turned their backs on him for the way in which he'd discredited Allah's name. Only his childhood friend, Mohamed, was he able to rely on. They'd both gone to school together, had both bitten in the same unripe mango. They'd bunked off school together. Bonds of friendship had turned into bonds of brotherhood. Mohamed's family welcomed him, to give him time to come up with a solution.

A year went by, but still, Hamed lived with his friend. During all that time, he'd hoped to find his Lydia. From time to time, he told himself that if he couldn't find the way of his heart, then perhaps, he needed to get back in touch with his family. Humiliate himself, beg his father for his forgiveness, beg his community for forgiveness for the way in which he disgraced Allah.

But then, what would happen if Lydia were to return with his child? Too afraid to solve that equation, he'd adopted a destructive behaviour and today, he was paying the price. Because he'd wanted a beautiful model on his arm, he'd reaped a lung cancer. Today, worn out by the illness, the hospital has become his second home. *What sorts of twists and turns of life were waiting for him in the future? What future?*

His future, his love and his health were so much upon his mind that he did not hear the doctor call him. The woman, whose child had left the toy lying on the ground, called out to him.

"Sir, it's your turn."

The Woman's Way

Catherine Shepherd

I see her from a distance, a lump of dark shadow high in the trees. Like a dwarf, puffed up. The owl calls into the bright night. My breath on the window steams up the glass. I rub the misty patch to see clearer. The moon is full and white. No hoot echoes back. We wait, the owl and I. Her partner is not around. To some in this valley she is death but to me she is the night. What I cannot see but what I know. The fire has burnt down, leaving orange coals. The air in the bedroom is cold and so I climb back into bed.

Francois turns to face me as I wobble the mattress.

"You can't sleep again?" he says, stretching his hands toward me.

My body stiffens.

Since that first night something strange happened to me. At first, I did not want to part from the silk and lace that draped my body because I believed the magic of that glorious day would disappear. As we fumbled in the sheets, the pain and blood were second to me wanting to please him. Francois helped himself to me in an unexpected way, like an animal slowly devouring its prey in candlelight. My mother's words about destiny didn't help. I could only answer his gruff requests by my physical self. No words were spoken. In the end we were just faded outlines on the ceiling. I couldn't feel my body any more, as if it was not my own.

Now, two years later, my shadows must curse me, for my body does not do what a farmer's wife should. We sit on the porch wall drinking coffee, watching the mountains turn streaky white with the rains. I chatter about the crops, as the steam of my cup rises in my face, about my dreams, about our future, but he bends down and takes my chin in his fingers and looks me straight in the eyes.

"Forget about the man jobs," he says, his finger sliding off my jaw. "I have asked you again and again to seek out Ma Rose. She threw the bones once for me."

I breathe in sharply.

"She is the one who can help us have a baby." He flicks a big green aphid off his sleeve, sighing. "They haven't left yet but will soon, winter is coming. Go to her."

I stand up and dust my apron. I won't indulge him by asking of the bones and the scattered message they left. Everyone knows that Ma Rose is the wise woman of these mountains. Ma Rose, the Seer, the healer, the baby maker, the love potion cook. Francois is looking at the ground, probably to see where the bug landed. Chin up. I march into the house to finish my coffee alone. I swear under my breath and throw clothes around the room.

"The new slave laws will destroy us yet," I shout out loud but know my voice will not make it down the stairs. All my favourite dresses are dirty. Susannah is neglecting me, but it is because I refuse help. It is not her fault. I search deep in my chest and pull out a musty white cotton frock with lace trim.

It is a fifteen-minute walk to the kraal. The mist is lifting along the river path and the sun heats up the top of my head as I walk through the papyrus forest. Ma Rose is under the fever tree. She greets me with her wrinkles and crooked smile, smelling of animal fat and oak-wood smoke. The aroma of strange herbs hangs in the air. The backdrop to the hut is the east view of the mountains with its many waterfalls that lie like white ribbons down a huge sleeping dragon's paw. At the top is where it all begins. The lifeblood of our fertile fields. On a clear day, at the end of the desert where her path starts before the great escarpment, she could, with our eyes perhaps, see the white beaches that rim the distant Indian seas.

"Come," Ma Rose says, calling me from my thoughts.

Grass baskets filled with bushels and little tin boxes pave the entrance. There is dried African lavender, chamomile and frankincense for healing; sweet buchu for pain and tobacco for fear.

"What has brought you here to Ma Rose? Your fortune? You have pain?" she asks.

"No." Tears sting my eyes. "It has been more than twenty-four moons, Ma Rose. Since our marriage in 1806. No child is coming. And also, I am dry. It is sore."

"My sweet girl." The old lady raises her head from the fire and looks at me. "I can help with the child. As for the burning," she turns back to the orange flames in the wood and ash, "you are like a brand-new well in hot sands waiting for rain. When was your last bleed, child?"

"A Sunday ago."

The lady squats down on the floor and pushes her palms into her old cheeks. She sits for a while with her eyes closed, her head nodding slowly. I wait in the warm hut. The little smoke there drifts around me, making shadows in the rays of light that find cracks through the reeds. Ma Rose opens her eyes.

"Next Monday, at first light, you will meet him by the grove behind the mill, with your face covered."

"Meet who?"

"A young herdsman to lie with. It will be quick. Engelbrecht's first wife was barren too. So you see, Izzy, it is the only way." She walks to me and gently places her rough hands on mine.

"But the colour," I blurt out the words. "The baby will not be Engelbrecht's; he will kill us."

Then I think of the act itself. The herb she has thrown on the fire makes my head spin. I clutch at a wooden beam near the entrance and start to gag. A lump of breakfast rises and sticks in my throat. I swallow it down and straighten up.

"Child, he will not kill his son or his beautiful wife. Perhaps he will even understand. The dreams have willed it, Isabella. They see no problems like your imaginings."

But I do. That Sunday night I have nightmares that leave my body moist when I wake from them in terror. Francois turns to soothe me and then slips off again into the world of dreams, leaving me staring into darkness. When he stirs a little later he tries to make love with me, but I feign all sorts of ailments, secretly thanking God for the gift of a great imagination. But he has had enough and takes me anyway. The tears are hot and I feel burnt down there. Closed and dry. I feel like a lady as old as Ma Rose.

In the early morning, in the still-dark room, I sense Francois watching me. He tugs me to him and we lie like spoons. When I hear him gently snoring, I slip away. The cold autumn air hangs around the farm as I run, pulling my shawl tight around my shoulders.

And so I go to lie with the herdsman at sunrise. It is just as she said it would be, and so much, much more. He is young and breathing. His face is wrapped with a soft cotton fabric that reminds me of pictures of ancient dead Egyptians from Oupa Engelbrecht's library. I wonder what I look like to him with a crude sack over my head. I see his watchful eyes, brown and beautiful. I don't love Francois but I am like a fox slyly toying with my life. I feel disgusted as it is love I want, not trickery. When he places his hand on my waist I want to scream and run but I cannot retreat from his touch.

I must have a son; it is my destiny.

The wild fig hairs flitter in the air below fast, shape-shifting clouds as I lie on the hard ground frozen from fright. I don't feel the cold; I hardly even feel the stinging. The rushing river captures my imagination. The pebbles rumble as they roll back and forth over each other. I could be a fish right now if I concentrate hard enough. I only open my eyes for brief moments to find new forms in white floating in the blue. When it is done all I hear is the crunching of leaves as he runs away and the squirrels calling to each other. I laugh out loud and then sob at the absurdity of having sex with an unknown man.

To soothe the rawness inside me, I walk in the stream on the way home, careful not to wash. Holding my dress above my waist, I let the cold water swirl around. The tears slow down but still slide off my chin and onto my neck dropping into the dark water below. They are warm and comforting and I let them fall as I catch my breath. I don't love Francois. I have never loved Francois. In the distance, I can hear a shepherd boy whistling to his goats as they meh-eh-eh under a pink sky turning orange with the sun.

Winter in the Langeberg comes and goes, enlightening the farm land to a harsh summer's spell and my belly swells. The waterfalls dry up, heather turns the mountains purple and the hammerhead bird fills its nest with a vigour similar to Francois'. Relentless, he carries on, building up the outhouse, chopping wood, ploughing clay-dense land, picking an orchard clean of nuts, stroking my firm dimpled thighs by the stream on picnic days. It is a good time, but I worry about the baby and I dream devilish images about my head and a noose and what betrayal can bring.

Thank God for Susannah. She comforts me through the long hot months. We walk together in the mountains picking brambleberries for jam. She teaches me how to boil their sweet fruit until it is perfect for bottling.

"Don't pull your nose up at the worms, Izzy; they burn away."

But I do, at the worms, at the heat and the flies. We pass the herds people in their summer kraal as we make our way to the sacred grove, where Susannah reads out loud from her old Persian book. The guttural consonances make me desire this author, Omar Khayyam. But I don't understand a word. Ma Rose comes to search for us beside the knotted tree trunks and smiles brightly each time I touch my stomach. We investigate the many caves that run along the gorge nearest to the farm and fish for eel. I turn bright red when I see young men from the kraal plopping melons in the river to use as decoys for the crocodiles, so we can swim in the warm water. I turn my nose up at their eyes when they glance at me. Fear can be a prideful look for some. I listen to the steps they take. To the sounds of their feet on the path.

The baby will arrive before the herdspeople leave for the Klein Karoo, before the mountains are thick with snow and the women climb the Tradouw Pass with the children and animals. On a misty day it looks like they are walking into the heavens from where I sit on the stoep. I pray it will not be my body hung in a tree they must pass when they begin their journey by our farm after the first cold rains. The men will take the route directly over the Langeberg Mountains. If the hunting is good on their journey, they will feast together when they reach the top by the hot waters.

But for now, it is only the sweltering heat we feel. My baby grows fat inside me, and I can hardly walk. Small dust storms appear on the grey rocky outcrops that lie in the distance. With the heat comes the chaos. Locust warnings keep Francois on edge. The dam is running low. The border river now just a snake of water. He paces around the house and fusses over me, but I smile half-heartedly, for truth be told, my nerves are shot.

"This is a big baby," Susannah says one humid afternoon as she sweeps and cooks and cleans my house. I can still waddle outside and throw the chickens their corn and barley husks. The pale grass is dying. I worry about Ma Rose and her gifts. The worry eats into me like worms, like those fat white summer-berry worms.

And so it is. One morning my waters break in such a torrent that a large puddle forms around my feet. Lumbering toward Susannah's room, half slipping in the wetness, holding the bottom of my heavy belly, I can barely whisper the words, "The baby is coming."

There are deathly cramps and Francois lamenting outside the door. Susannah wipes the sweat from my brow. And the window. I keep looking out the window. The bright sun and blue sky cast watery mirages on the grey far-away cliffs. Waterfalls, I think. "Rain is coming," I say.

"And so is this hunk of a baby," mutters Susannah.

I grow more delirious but I know to push and push, so I do, creeping in agony on the bed till I am half over the edge on all fours. Then I split. The baby arrives, bloody and screaming. From the corner of my eye I see Susannah holding him, a white-haired, blue-eyed baby. Francois bangs on the door.

"It is a boy, Master Engelbrecht. You have a son," Susannah says; she is shaking but her voice is loud and strong.

I hear the shouts of joy, but my body tells me to stay and push on. Something is wrong. The cramps get worse. I whisper to Susannah, "It is coming."

Then it slides out, quick and slimy, into Susannah's hands just before the afterbirth thuds and splatters on the floor. Susannah holds in a sob, but it comes out anyway. He is so tiny, his brown body moving delicately. His eyes are closed but his head waves in his search for milk.

"My God!" I scream, covering my mouth with shaking hands.

"Quiet, girl," Susannah puts her face to mine, her eyes wide.

"How is it possible?" I whisper.

"What have you done, Izzy?" she replies, turning her head from me and grabbing at skins and cloths.

She wraps up the baby and holds its mouth to my nipple to stop it from crying. He squirms on my chest and latches, his tiny lips taking in everything. There is a flowing sensation in my left breast as my milk begins to flow. I watch clear liquid spread out his mouth over my nipple. My other son screams. Engelbrecht is shouting at the door. There is knocking. Banging.

"I want to see my son. Ladies, Izzy, *now*!"

"Yes, in a minute. I am just cleaning up." Susannah speaks with a calmness that echoes in the chaos of the room. I vomit quietly into a bowl.

Susannah takes the baby from me and gently places him in her blouse. She scoops up some of the bloody cloths and holds them in a bundle over her lumpy chest, opening the door.

"Go ahead." She waves her free hand in a grand gesture for Francois to enter.

He is beaming. Radiant. The door closes behind him, leaving us alone.

During the night I wake to suckle my baby. When he cries from fullness, I wrap my new son in his swaddling blanket and tip-toe with him downstairs to Susannah's room. I am desperate for answers. The light of my lantern in my free hand illuminates the stone corridor that leads through the kitchen to the back rooms. It is icy cold and I walk awkwardly, the blood still seeping through my cloths. It is a small room housing one chest, a side table with a porcelain jug and a small bed, now empty. I open the chest with my foot. Slowly lifting the latch with my toes and firmly kicking it open. The baby stirs in the crook of my arm. Peering into the shadows, I can see all her clothes are missing. Just strange letters by old Omar Khayyam stare back at me from the book cover. I can only guess she will attempt the pass in order to catch up with the others.

The next morning Francois is like a mad man when he discovers Susannah's disappearance along with her horse. He believes she is jealous of our baby but he won't issue a price on her head.

"Slave or no slave," he glares at me while I lie sobbing in my bed, "I will let your friend go as she likes, but I hope you have learnt your lesson about trust?"

I am tormented. My beautiful son suckles on me, thirsty for milk but all I can do is obsess about my broken life through my bedroom window. I see the young herdsman running away into the woods. The scene runs over and over in my mind like the spokes of the mill. What else is there for me to do? A new mother can hardly move from her baby and bed in the early days. The vultures that circle above the empty gorges terrify me. What is calling the birds to feast? I pray to my God that it is neither my Susannah nor my other love they eat. It is destiny that they make it to the top. I keep hearing the crushing of leaves. He had a gentle touch. Like the feeling when he left. Whispers of someone light on their feet and in their heart.

And what of me? A year to the day. A mystical night's end lures me to seek out this other world, while everyone still sleeps. A flap of wings by the open window stops my breath. It is just the owl. I can see her peering in. Her quick head movements and huge eyes blinking. What is it that I know already? I exhale slowly, adding to my already heightened sense. I can't shake my adventurous dreams. Ma Rose is holding a baby neatly swaddled in a red-velvet cloth. She is laughing and chanting. A body in the shadows is flicking water onto them. The droplets morph into vapour and like a shroud covers the figures. I cannot see the baby but I can hear cheerful gurgling. I must do something. My son and new slave woman lie in their cot in the *voorkamer*. I walk quietly past them. Susannah's replacement is also his wet nurse, so even if the child is thirsty, Francois will not be woken.

I step out into cool air, thankful for my warm coat and boots.

The brightening dawn light and morning birds lighten my mood for the first time in weeks. I run. Clumps of grass and uneven stones rise up at me from the path as I fixate on my nimble feet and hear the water gurgle as it plummets from the mill's pipes into the well and beyond. A thin white mist sticks over the stream that comes from yonder. Out of breath, I sit beside the small tower and listen to the trickle of water.

I hear goats. Then I see him. On the other side of the river. He is standing so still that for a moment he resembles a ghost wearing a gown of fog. When he steps forward I see he has a leopard skin pulled around his torso. He beckons me to come to him with his hands and then smiles. I recognise him from around these parts. Why has he not left with the others? My heart races and my breath quickens. I climb through the river unsteadily on the pebbles. This drought has sucked the river, so it is easy to cross now. When I jump onto the earth from a rock he takes my hands in his. *I know those eyes.*

"We have a child but I don't know where he is," I say, my voice thick as I drop my hands from his.

"I do, our son is at the Mission Station. The Pastor found him one morning on his *stoep*. Don't worry," he strokes my hair, his eyes searching mine, "no one knows the baby's origin."

I fold my arms tight against my stomach to stop from shivering.

"And what of Susannah?"

He shakes his head slowly. I begin to sob. The tears have now reached my lip and I flick my tongue to lick them away. A few minutes pass, the two of us face each other below the wild fig trees, as the sun begins to rise over the distant hills.

"How did you know I would come today? Did you remember?" I speak so softly he has to move closer to hear me.

"I am here every day, Isabella. I bring the goats to drink at first light." He reaches for my face, his fingers touching my cheek.

"Oh, quite right, they should never have to go thirsty."

And then we kiss. I don't know who starts it but I shake like a leaf in a *berg* wind. It is a long, wild kiss. From deep within myself an unknown wetness stirs.

"What will happen to us all?" I choke on the words as I push him away.

"Nothing bad," he says. "Ma Rose, my mother, has dreamed it."

I steady myself and step back. "I may just walk this way again," I mutter in the warming air and turn for the house. I need not look back for I know how he stands. Tall and smiling, the rising sun at his back.

Afterword

Bwesigye Bwa Mwesigire

In 2013, when we published our first anthology, *Picture Frames and other stories*, comprising fourteen short stories that had been long listed for the first ever Writivism Short Story Prize, despite our ambition, we did not have a clear picture of the future of publishing prize fiction. The idea of holding a workshop, followed by publishing an anthology and a short story prize was inspired by the Caine Prize for African Writing. One of us had attended a previous Caine prize workshop in Kenya, and had appeared in that year's Caine Prize anthology. Another had once been shortlisted for the Caine Prize for African Writing, and therefore her story included in the annual anthology. The annual Caine Prize anthology publishes both workshop fiction and prize fiction.

In 2012, when the Writivism Literary Initiative was launched in Kampala, the annual Caine Prize anthology was the surest regular annual collection of short fiction by African writers working in English. The other outlets for regular annual short fiction were journals and magazines. The Farafina magazine had long folded, and the Farafina Trust creative writing workshop did not have an annual anthology by its participants. Kwani?, the journal, like Chimurenga Chronic, were published whenever they were published, and they are more than just anthologies. Their digital counterparts like Saraba and Bakwa Magazine among others fell in the same category. They are periodicals for all intents and purposes but whose missions go beyond short fiction. We saw the Writivism annual anthology of short stories as strictly a prize fiction book. It would be different from the spasmodic Jalada, or Afridiaspora, or even Brittle Paper anthologies, which emerged on the scene later.

In our understanding, the annual Writivism anthology would be tied to the short story prize, and as long as we would run the prize annually, we would publish the anthology, too. *Picture Frames and other stories* (2013), *Fire in the Night and other stories* (2014) and *Roses for Betty and other stories* (2015) have been published in the tradition of African prize fiction. All the short stories included in the above anthologies were long listed for the annual Writivism prize for short fiction. In 2015, we decided to widen our publishing beyond prize fiction. Our activities as an initiative, for example workshops and online mentoring were producing creative work that we loved, some of which would fall off the radar, as the prize would not recognise all the stories that came through these programmes. The prize is open to all emerging writers, whether they attended our workshop or / and mentoring programme or not. We started to publish a mini-anthology of short fiction, in digital format, in collaboration with partners to include stories from our other programmes, besides the prize.

My Maths Teacher Hates Me and other stories (2015), and *Your Heart Will Skip A Beat and other stories* (2016) have been published in the series in collaboration with Jalada, and Bahati Books respectively. The first of these digital mini-anthologies attracted the attention of Nick Mulgrew, a writer, critic, and publisher. In a review essay, written for Chimurenga Chronic Books, he categorised the short stories in the anthology alongside those in Lusaka Punk and other stories (the Caine Prize anthology for that year) as competition fiction. Mulgrew's label of competition fiction, while generally true, isn't entirely accurate of the process through which both *My Maths Teacher Hates Me and other stories* and *Lusaka Punk and other stories* emerge. The former is not necessarily compiled from a competition. The stories are picked from the workshops and mentoring. The Caine Prize anthologies on their hand combine workshopped stories with those shortlisted for the prize in a given year.

Mulgrew's competition fiction label, could however apply to the

Writivism annual anthologies, published in print and digital formats, comprising only long listed stories for the Writivism prize. I would still be uncomfortable with the word 'competition' to describe the prize. A literary prize is more than just a competition or even a contest. While there is money attached to winning the prize, while there are opportunities some people get and others do not, when they win the prize, there is much more that is lost when we reduce a prize to a competition. A prize is a community. A prize is a family. Everyone whose creative work engages with the prize is part of this community. To reduce it to competition means that it is a case of winners and losers, because that is what happens when there is competition. Some win, some lose. Literature and culture are not competitive endeavours in that way.

The process that makes the Writivism Prize is more important than the results. It is more than the winning stories, the shortlisted stories, and the long listed stories. Everyone who engages with it, is influenced by it and influences it. Emerging writers give generously, the gift of their art: administrators, readers and judges, also donate generously their nurturing and appreciative spirits to the work presented before them, and editors of the anthology add their concentration and skill to bring the best out of the stories. This is a process one can't reduce to a competition. While the label, 'prize fiction' is itself not apt, it is more suitable than 'competition'. Prize fiction is more than the prize cash. It is more than the monetary value of the perks of winning the prize.

Tinuke Adeyi, writing for Book Wawa, about our most recent anthology until this one you are holding in your hands, *Roses for Betty and other stories*, identifies the other important value of prize fiction. She writes:

> *Home-grown short-story [prizes] are essential to the continued growth of the African literary scene, and their existence assures us of writers and readers who will shape the African narrative. To this extent,* Roses for Betty *gets full marks. More than the stories themselves,*

it is the commitment of the writers to the evolution of craft, and the willingness of some of them to explore new themes that warms the heart. Sometimes, the journey is as important as the destination.

The Writivism Literary Initiative is primarily interested in the consolidation of an African-owned, Africa-based literary and cultural industry. All our activities, be they workshops, online mentoring, the various prizes we run, school visits and the annual festival we organise in Kampala, share that singular purpose. It is not enough for us to tell our stories. To show our stories. It is important to own the means of production for this industry of storytelling and showing. That is not the entire picture either. While it is important too, that we own the means of production of our stories elsewhere, away from the geography of our continent, it is even more important that we own and control the industry at home. The activism in the name of the initiative, Writivism is the advocacy for this autonomy. We work together with as many initiatives as possible, what separates us from many is our perspective, our purpose and our activities. You can't separate the processes through which the anthology you are holding in your hands comes together, from the stories you have just read.

Sundown is special because it is the first anthology that we are publishing in print in collaboration with an Africa-based, African-owned independent publisher, Black Letter Media. *Sundown* is also special because as you have read, it is the first anthology that comprises short fiction, creative nonfiction and poetry. This is a result of the introduction of a new prize for creative nonfiction, the Koffi Addo prize and the one off Okot p Bitek prize for poetry in translation. We have kept our regular anthology free of thematic requirements for writers. The prizes we run are not thematic on purpose. This we believe allows for the imaginative freedom of the writer. It is rare to have stories as wildly imaginative as Sundown in themed competitions. Whether a writer chooses to confront a big theme, or to indulge in stylistic gymnastics, is a choice the Writivism prize leaves to them. Our judges do not have criteria that requires a certain way of writing, or certain themes. It is this freedom that we believe lies at the centre of the creative endeavour. We hope you have enjoyed the stories and poems in this anthology.

Contributors' Bios

ACAN INNOCENT IMMACULATE is a 21-year old Ugandan pursuing a Bachelor's degree in Medicine and Surgery. Writing has always been her first love and she looks forward to a literary atmosphere where African stories will break the mould even more than they do now. Acan is the winner of the 2016 Writivism Short Story Prize.

YVETTE TETTEH (b. 1992) is a British-born Ghanaian artist, yoga teacher, and aspiring farmer. She holds a BA in Cultural Anthropology, and French, from Stanford University (CA, USA.) Her work is centred on the black body, and the intersection of intimacy, reserve, and performativity. Her astrological signs are: Cancer Sun, Aries Moon, and Gemini in Ascendant. Yvette is based in Accra, Ghana and is the winner of the Koffi Addo Prize for Creative Non Fiction.

GLORIA MWANIGA ODARY is a high school teacher in Baringo where she also runs a children's reading club. She is also a freelance writer of literary pieces for the Saturday Nation and the East African newspapers as well as coordinator of Amka, a literary workshop that meets monthly at the Goethe Institut in Nairobi to critique works by budding female writers in Kenya. Boyi, shortlisted for the 2016 Writivism Prize was her first attempt at writing a short story.

LAURE GNAGBÉ BLÉDOU: Passionate, woman, lover, mother, daughter, sister, cousin, friend, Africa-ddict, thirty-something, impatient, Ivorian, French, human, reader, speaker, writer, demanding, citizen, vegetarian, traveller, road-trip fan, learner, book-lover, bridge-lover, chocolate-lover, music enthusiast, sharer, feminist, old-school, new-school, journalist, @laurebledou.

AITO OSEMEGBE JOSEPH works as a Sales Professional during the day and at dusk, writes horror stories and psychological thrillers. His short stories have appeared in 'Brittle Paper' and 'Kalahari Review'.

He is set to publish a collection of short stories and is currently working on his debut novel.

ABU AMIRAH finds pleasure in the written word because of the ability to lose himself in an infectious world filled with characters begging to come to life, metaphors, muse and madness; and amid all this, the power to give the reader permission to laugh, cry, love and hate!

GBENGA ADESINA, Nigerian poet and essayist, jointly won the 2016 Brunel African Poetry Prize. His poem, "How To Paint A Girl" was selected by Mathew Zapruder for its "clarity of observation and empathetic insight into the suffering of another" for the *New York Times*. He has received fellowships and scholarships from the Norman Mailer Poetry, Fine Arts Work Centre, Provincetown, The Open Society Foundation in Goree Island, off the coast of Senegal, Poets House New York and Callaloo at Oxford. His poetry chapbook, *Painter of Water*, was published in the New Generation African Poetry series and his poetry manuscript, *Holy Bodies* was a finalist for the 2017 Sillerman First Book Prize.

OKWUDILI NEBEOLISA: born in 1993, is a Nigerian writer whose works have appeared (or will be featured) in Threepenny Review, Commonwealth Writers, Beloit Poetry Journal, Cincinnati Review, Salamander Magazine, Lambda Review, Ruminate Magazine, Ambit Magazine, and elsewhere. He was a 2016 Ebedi Fellow at the Ebedi International Writers Residency and was a finalist for the 2016 Sillerman First Book Prize for African Poets and the 2014 Raedleaf Poetry Prize in the international category. He won the Jalada Prize for African Literature in the Poetry category.

FARAI MUDZINGWA is a small-town boy who writes sometimes, and irreverently, from Harare. He has articles published in The Zimbabwean, The Africa Report, Africa Is A Country, NBO Press, and, short stories in Kwani? Uchaguzi '13, and the Weaver Press collections - "Writing Lives" (2nd Ed.) and "Writing Mystery & Mayhem."

LE K-YANN (Yann-Stevi Tsiku Kheme) is a language student at the Institut Superieur Pedagogique of Gombe – Kinshasa in the DRC. Le K-Yann writes slam, poetry, short stories, and essays and is currently working on a novel. He has taken part in national and international competitions and can be found at the various cultural centres of Kinshasa reading or writing.

IDZA LUHUMYO is a Kenyan writer.

MEGAN ROSS is a writer, journalist and poet from the Eastern Cape in South Africa. She is the second runner up of the 2016 Short Story Day Africa prize. Her work has appeared in Prufrock, Aerodrome, Itch and several anthologies. She is also a Miles Morland Writing Scholarship Shortlistee and the winner of the Iceland Writers Retreat Alumni Award.

PRAISE NABIMANYA is a preacher's daughter. Her family, friends and God are the reason she lives. Words are her life. They keep her grounded. When she is sad or happy, she writes. When she is too excited or anxious, she reads to find her calm.

JUDE MUTUMA is a lover of life and a lover of books, who sometimes has a hard time telling the two apart. Currently, he is a finalist Communication student at the Jomo Kenyatta University of Agriculture and Technology. His work has previously been published on the Jalada-Writivism anthology 'My Math Teacher Hates Me and other stories.'

DOREEN ANYANGO is a Ugandan writer. Her short fiction has appeared in several online publications such as Wordrite, Lawino and the Kalahari Review; as well as in print in the latest FEMRITE anthology Nothing To See Here. She is currently working on a collection of stories and her first novel.

BURA-BARI NWILO, a photo enthusiast and screenwriter was born in Port Harcourt, Nigeria in 1987. He studied English and Literature at the University of Nigeria, Nsukka. Nwilo draws inspiration from his good and bad childhood experiences, of bloody cult clashes in his secondary school to a fond long trek home.

FRANCES OGAMBA is a language graduate from the University of Nigeria, Nsukka. She writes in French and English and works with a shipping company in Port Harcourt, Nigeria. She models and dances among other pursuits of diverse ingenuity.

SESE YANE lives and works in Kilifi County, Kenya. His short stories and poems have appeared in The Kalahari Review, Short Story Day Africa and Apex Book of World Fiction SF4.

NOELLA MOSHI is a Tanzanian living in Lagos. She is a social entrepreneur, aspiring philosopher, and lover of beautiful words.

ACIDRI MALUNGA is a Ugandan writer and law student. He was awarded the MACOSA prize for best student in English in 2010. He writes articles and short stories in his free time.

KOUADIO KOUAKOU is an Ivoirien writer.

CATHERINE SHEPHERD was born in South Africa (1970) and graduated from Rhodes (1992). The end of Apartheid was the highlight of her youth. Inspired by Rachel Zadok and Writivism her stories have been published in anthologies including 'My Holiday Shorts' (2013), 'My Maths Teacher Hates Me' and 'Imagine Africa 500' (2015).

About Writivism

Writivism is a Kampala-based initiative that promotes African Literature through literary prizes as well as an annual workshops and mentoring programme for emerging writers who live in African countries. In the past, Writivism directly published anthologies arising out of the above programmes. Six titles have been published so far including: Picture Frames and other stories (2013), Fire in the Night and other stories (2014), My Maths Teacher Hates Me and other stories (2015), Roses for Betty and other Stories (2015), Your Heart will Skip a Beat and other Stories (2016) and Daughters who Become Lovers and other Stories (2017). Sundown and other Stories is the seventh and first to be published and distributed in collaboration with Black Letter Media.

Writivism also curates an annual literary festival in Kampala that hosts top contemporary African writers, thinkers, publishers, journalists, academics and other figures in the literary world. Over 500 of these have attended the previous four editions of the festival engaging a combined in person and online audience of over 5000 people. Activities at the festival range from school visits, book launches, panel discussions, exhibitions, stage plays, and annual awards event for the Writivism prize winners among others.

Writivism was founded as the first programme of the Centre for African Cultural Excellence (CACE), a non-profit that promotes African ideas and freedom through the arts and culture. You can find more information about Writivism at www.writivism.org and www.writivism.com.

The Team